3 0063 00382 7567

Eastern   Apr 2022

D1776836

This item no longer belongs to Davenport Public Library

FRIENDS
of the
Davenport Public Library

"Celebrate The Printed Word"
Endowment Fund
provided funds for the
purchase of this item

Subterranean Press 2021

Square³ Copyright © 2021
by Seanan McGuire.
All rights reserved.

Dust jacket illustration Copyright © 2021
by Julie Dillon.
All rights reserved.

Interior design Copyright © 2021
by Desert Isle Design, LLC.
All rights reserved.

Edited by Yanni Kuznia

First Edition

ISBN
978-1-64524-053-2

Subterranean Press
PO Box 190106
Burton, MI 48519

subterraneanpress.com

Manufactured in the United States of America

For Carrie and Doc.
You change the laws of physics, my dear ones.

 **POSITIVE INTEGER I: BACKGROUND**

CHAPTER 1: INCURSION

1.1.

When the first holes ripped in the fabric of reality and the first interlopers appeared, looming out of the sudden unseasonable fog like mountains or wayward aircraft, no one knew what to expect. The world was not braced. There had been no warning—

(or if there had been warning, it had been too diffuse to help. In the months and years to come, people would point to a dozen possible causes for the disaster, each as likely and reasonable as any of the others. A record-breaking particle accelerator had been turned on in Siberia; a long-range space mission had returned to Earth; several solar storms had caused massive electromagnetic disruptions; a mathematician working in hyperspatial mathematics intended to map the movement of parallel dimensions had logged multiple breakthroughs within the weeks leading directly up to the event. None of these incidents were conclusive, and none of them could ever be proven connected)

—and no way to predict the event. One moment, nature had laws and generally followed them, unenforced and unpoliced. One moment, everything was normal. The next, physics and mathematics were negotiable things, and the supposed laws that had always governed biology were shattered beyond all repair.

1.2.

IT WAS MAY when it began. That, at least, we know to be non-negotiable; time, outside of specific and well-defined exceptions, has remained the same even in the aftermath of everything that's happened.

It can't be called "a beautiful morning in May," although it was, in some locations; it was also "a freezing night in May" and "a stormy afternoon in May," and every other combination of weather and climate and time that can be reasonably assembled. But it was May, and in North America, in the state of Illinois, in the city of Evanston, just outside Chicago, it was a beautiful morning.

Evanston was one of those cities that sprang up after the urbanization of America, not quite part of the major population hub, not rural, and not far enough out to be considered suburban. It was small enough to be comfortable and self-policing, while still connected to Chicago proper by trains and bus routes. Chicago's infrastructure supplied most of the city's needs, and most of the people who chose to live there were happy with small yards and close quarters, choosing a reduction of personal space over a reduction of available amenities.

No one has ever been able to firmly prove a correlation between the holes—more properly referred to as "rifts" by most members of the scientific community, although no one has ever provided a compelling argument for why this is a more accurate term than the common "hole"—and the density of urban areas, but the pattern, inchoate and chaotic as it seemed in the beginning, quickly became clear once a little distance was achieved and information could be collated:

Every single rift opened in or near a population center of at least seventy thousand people. And each of them was within twenty miles (thirty-two kilometers) of a population center of at least two million people. Cities of seventy thousand without a larger city inside that radius were spared, as were smaller cities within the radius.

(Scientists have been arguing since the first incursion that this doesn't prove the rifts were targeted in any way: it's purely mathematical, and a reaction to the density of all the little accessories of humanity, not only the human lives, but the technology, the cars, the buildings, even the concrete. Without further data, it's impossible to prove things either way, and given what further data would require, even the people who most want the answer have reason to hope they'll never have it.)

But it was a beautiful morning in Evanston, Illinois, on May sixteenth, twenty twenty-two, when the sky—which had been a beautiful shade of placid eggshell blue, without a single cloud in sight—suddenly turned the variegated, oceanic green that signaled the approach of a tornado, one that had somehow managed to avoid showing up on any weather systems or long-range radar detectors. Clouds began to swirl across the sky, accumulating with a speed anyone who had lived in the region for any length of time knew to fear.

And still the sirens didn't go off, and still no warnings were issued. Parents shouted for their children (only recently released from the grips of a global pandemic that had snatched away almost two full years of their lives) to come inside, and the children, with regretful, resentful glances at the sky, gathered up their balls and bicycles and toys and did as they were told. Phones rang as people called their loved ones at work and begged them to come home, fearing the wrath of what would surely be a once-in-a-lifetime storm.

(The phrase was losing all meaning as people continued to apply it to each storm that came on larger than the one before, but with more and more frequency. What had once been genuinely "once in a lifetime" was now more like "once in a season" as the big storms came with increasing frequency, thanks to a changing climate changing the weather at the same time.)

And near the cemetery, two girls, one seventeen, the other a bright-eyed fourteen, stopped their bikes and looked up at the sky.

"Mom's going to want us home," said the older, with the disappointed air of the one who knew she was expected to be the responsible daughter and take care of her little sister, despite still being a child herself.

"Mom should let us have cellphones if she wants us to come home as soon as it gets a little windy," countered the younger tartly, and started to pedal, riding deeper into the cemetery and leaving her sister with little choice but to follow if she wanted to keep her in sight.

"Susan!" the older yelled, pedaling as hard as she could. The sky was growing steadily greener, taking on a hue she'd never seen before, bright and almost glassy in its unblemished clarity. The gathering clouds were dark and stormy, but somehow they didn't interfere with the sight of that improbable sky. "Susan, come *back* here!"

"Make me!" shouted her sister, and kept pedaling.

They had survived two years locked up in the same house, waiting for vaccination and social behavioral patterns to get the COVID-19 pandemic under control, and they had come out of it still friends, which was far better than many of the siblings they knew had been able to manage. They genuinely liked each other. Susan liked how seriously Katharine approached her life, liked the way her older sister listened and observed and did her best to understand. She wasn't a stick in the mud—far from it—but she knew the consequences of her actions before she took them, and had to be persuaded to break rules, no matter how arbitrary. Maybe that would have been a foundation for dislike, but she was *willing* to be persuaded, *willing* to listen to the reasons that a specific rule was pointless, or arbitrary, or unnecessary. Having a sister with a keen analytical mind who only felt absolutely compelled to follow the rules she believed made sense had always been an asset to Susan.

And Katharine, who was the way she was because she genuinely didn't know any other way to be, and couldn't be a spontaneous rulebreaker or a spontaneous troublemaker even if she tried, admired and adored the way her younger sister seemed to do whatever she liked, and damn the consequences. Susan was clever enough to understand the difference between gambling with dessert or an extra hour of television time and actual danger, something that Katharine had never quite been able to internalize; for her, all bad consequences were the same, while Susan weighed and measured them on a scale of her own making, and misbehaved with gleeful abandon whenever the scales came out in a way she found acceptable. They were sisters and they were friends and while the pandemic had weakened their bonds with many of their peers (Katharine not having had a large number of close friends even before two years of virtual hangouts and no school-enforced social time, Susan having been of an age and disposition where making the transition to a completely online social life hadn't come as easily to her as might have been expected), they still liked each other, and they liked the roles they played in one another's lives:

Susan broke rules, and Katharine brought her back before she could hurt herself. When they were together they found a kind of balance between them, one that allowed them to keep going far longer than either of them could have managed on their own.

But that sky…something in Katharine recoiled from that sky, which was rapidly approaching a color she had never seen before, not even on news reports about historic storms. There was something alien and unnatural about it, terrifying in a way she didn't know how to identify or name.

"Susie, come *back!*" she howled, voice half-stolen by the whipping of the wind. "I really mean it! We have to get home! This is a *safety light!*"

They didn't think of "safety light" as a safe word, a phrase both of them had encountered and viewed with vague suspicion as something with inherently adult overtones, but they understood the concept of safe words as things that could be used in non-sexual situations, between family members, friends, and anyone who might need to call someone back from the edge of doing something dangerous. The sisters had stumbled into the principle several years earlier, when they watched a movie about women who fought ghosts and saved the world.

It was a throw-away line, a joke, but it had made Katharine squirm on the couch, visibly uncomfortable. Susan had turned to her.

"What's wrong?"

Within the family, Susan had long since taken on the role of "the Kitty whisperer," understanding her sister's moods and reactions better than either of their parents, better than any of

Katharine's schoolmates, who teased her and laughed at her discomfort and called her names Susan knew, because she'd heard them, but that were never spoken in the presence of their parents. Their parents, who had refused to have Katharine evaluated for autism out of the misguided belief that they'd just be "slapping a label on her for something she's going to grow out of anyway" and never quite understood that the lack of a label meant their oldest daughter wouldn't get access to services and privileges that would have helped her immensely. Their parents, who didn't *want* the task of playing interlocutor for their often perplexing older child, and were happy to leave it to their younger daughter, saddling Susan with a feeling of responsibility far beyond her years, and never saw anything wrong with this arrangement.

Katharine had squirmed on the couch further before she explained, somewhat haltingly, "Safety lights are for *everyone*. Safety lights tell you if something might be dangerous, and not telling someone when something might be dangerous is just the same as lying to them. If you're going to go into a lab, or a mechanic's shop, or anyplace where they're doing science or engineering, you should know when you're near dangerous things. Pretending that they aren't dangerous so you can go on doing whatever you want isn't…it isn't *fair*. People who want us to trust them should be *fair*."

Susan had looked at her scowling sister and felt herself almost overwhelmed with the need to protect her from a world that wasn't always going to give her safety lights, wasn't always going to let her know when she was walking into something dangerous. Their parents had already all but abdicated from the job of taking care of Kitty: they only took care of Susan because she was younger and more "normal" according to their narrow expectations of what their child would be. If someone was going to keep Kitty safe, Susan was it. There wasn't anyone else looking for the job.

"So we'll have safety lights, you and me," she'd said, grabbing Katharine's hand and holding it tightly, like she could be the anchor that kept her sister from sinking even deeper into a private nightmare. "If something's really dangerous—honestly dangerous, not breaking a rule or something you think I shouldn't be doing—all you need to do is tell me it's a safety light, and I'll stop. Right away, no questions asked, I'll stop. Every time."

"Really?" Katharine had asked, wiping tears off her cheeks with the back of her free hand and staring at Susan with wide, focused eyes.

Susan had nodded, and that had been that: their safety word was set, their rule was ironclad, and even now, even on the far side of the nightmares of lockdown and shared trauma, it was the one rule Susan had never tried to test or violate.

For a moment, Katharine was afraid the wind was already too strong, and her sister was already too far away, and wouldn't hear her. Then Susan slowed, stopping her bike. Katharine did the same. They looked at each other from a distance of less than twenty feet. (Seventeen point five, the scientists would confirm later.)

"Are you sure?" called Susan.

Katharine nodded vigorously, taking one hand off her handlebars and pointing to the sky. "That's not normal! It's not *natural!* We don't have to go home, but we have to get to cover as soon as we can!"

Susan nodded, accepting that her sister wouldn't lie to her using their secret phrase, and began pedaling toward Katharine, slowly and reluctantly, but moving in what they both believed to be the right direction. She wanted to be free, to feel the wind in her hair and see the sky above her, but she didn't want to die, and she knew that if they got caught out in the storm, they'd both be grounded for a week.

She was only ten feet away when the air between them ripped and tore like tissue paper, sparking with the blue-white flash of tiny sparks of nuclear fission as the very molecules were ripped in two, the clear view of the cemetery, of her *sister*, replaced with an infinite void. It was an almost velvety black, so dark it stole all the light from the world, at least until oil slick rainbows began to dance across it, filled with colors she had never seen before and could never describe after the fact.

(The colors of the rifts would prove to come through on camera, and scientists analyzing the data would later find that somehow, the presence of the rifts stimulated parts of the human brain in heretofore impossible ways, allowing the people who stared into them to see the forbidden colors—colors humanity lacked the physical adaptations to see. "I finally saw the world the way a mantis shrimp sees it," said one marine biologist, wiping his glasses idly on his shirt. "I'd always wanted to, and now I have, and I am so very, very sorry."

He was found dead in his lab three weeks later, his eyes—which he had gouged out with a sharpened spoon—floating in a nearby basin of water. He had died from shock and blood loss, but his widow would go on to say that he had really died of grief, mourning the loss of colors he had never been meant to possess.)

The rift shimmered. The rift danced. The rift gaped wider and wider, opening in a straight line that cut through the heart of Evanston, until a creature stepped through, its massive foot ending only inches shy of where Susan stood frozen astride her bike, staring open-mouthed at the nightmare unfolding in front of her.

The thing was easily sixty feet tall (the Evanston incursion featured one of the smaller interlopers, in line with the other incursions centered on smaller metro areas; this data point has been held up as proof that the correlation between density of human habitation and likelihood of an incursion is accurate), and the first thought her fear-addled mind could put together was, "Pokémon are *real*," because it looked like nothing so much as one of the legendary Pokémon, somehow ripped out of the cartoons and walking in the world.

The first law of Pokémon, as anyone who had ever encountered the franchise could tell you, was "you *do not* fuck with the legendary Pokémon." This one, while unlicensed by the

Nintendo Corporation, had the same vaguely familiar body form she had come to know and love in the pocket monsters, something like a toad somehow hybridized with a gorilla. Its skin was a deep, rubbery blue, and she could see the tiny fissures in its surface, little cracks that made it look as textured and realistic as she did.

It was real. She could smell it, too, the hot, rancid smell of flesh that had been rubbing against itself for far too long without being washed, underscored by an almost acidic sweetness that burned her nose and mouth. Susan began to gag, doubling over. That probably saved her life.

The creature continued emerging from the rift, and its tail passed less than a foot over Susan's head. If she'd been upright, it would have handily decapitated her. She and her bicycle fit neatly in the space between its massive feet as it strode past, long, kangaroo-esque tail swaying behind it as a counterbalance. Every step it took shook the ground, unpleasant vibrations that seemed like they must be shattering the creature's bones.

Susan straightened as it passed, when the smell diminished and she could breathe again, twisting to stare after it as it stomped into the distance, heading—as she would find out later, when she was collected by a rescue crew—for Chicago, where it would die a quick and probably painless death at the claws of the larger creature, its head ripped from its shoulders and hurled carelessly into the path of a nearby commuter train. The human deaths from that day would far outweigh the creature deaths, both in terms of number and in sheer mass. Each beast weighed tons. The piles of human corpses weighed more.

It opened its mouth and roared, a primal, terrible sound that shook the world even more than its footsteps, and Susan shuddered, glad only that it was moving away from her.

Away from *them*.

She turned and stared into the rift, suddenly remembering her sister. It continued to pulse and glisten, unchanging, and she thought for a moment of charging through it, letting momentum carry her across whatever void it contained.

She couldn't move. She could barely breathe. She was looking through a portal into some terrifying infinity, and whatever it contained—even if what it contained was Kitty, whom she loved more than anything, who she would happily have died any normal, comprehensible death for—was forbidden. She knew that down to the soles of her feet, and she couldn't move.

In the distance, the creature roared again. Susan let go of her handlebars and wailed, clapping her hands over her ears. Her bike fell to the side, taking her down with it, and she hit the pavement hard, banging her elbow on the cement and scraping the skin from her hands. Tears stung her eyes, blurring her vision, and when she finished blinking them away, the rift was gone.

The rest of Evanston had gone with it.

The demarcation was as stark if it had been done with a protractor, a hard black line scorched into the ground where the rift had been, and on the other side, a nightmare landscape of twisted, burning shapes, trees distorted into geometric nightmares, buildings collapsed, or going down in flames, or bent into angles that hurt the eye.

Katharine was nowhere to be seen.

Susan picked herself up from the ground and took a shaking step toward the line, then another, and another, but when she reached it, she couldn't step over it into that twisted world with no sister in sight. Her body refused to obey the command to keep moving. Instead, she stood frozen, put her hands over her eyes and sobbed.

1.3.

PEOPLE WHO SUFFERED direct exposure to a rift on the Earth side have reported complications ranging from short-term nausea, hallucinations, and disorientation, to full-bore breaks with reality, seeing rifts in every shadow, and eventual inability to cope with life outside full-time psychological care. Children are less likely to suffer long-term psychological effects, although children who suffered direct exposure are very likely to have lost family or loved ones on the other side, which carries with it its own psychological scarring.

Susan spent almost an hour standing by the line, while the sky above her, but not above the blackened sphere that had swallowed her sister and her city, cleared and returned to a sunshiny blue, while the sound of screams and sirens echoed from the parts of Evanston that were still Evanston, and not some new, nightmarish world, while Katharine didn't return. She watched the blackened world as much as she could, watched the trees burn without collapsing and the buildings—she assumed they were buildings—grow taller, putting out new arms and new angles, and Katharine didn't return.

No matter how hard she looked, she never saw her sister. She never saw anything move.

Eventually, when she was cold and hurt and sick from crying and fear, she returned to her bicycle, picked it up off the ground, slung her leg over the frame, and began pedaling away from the hard, curving edge of the demarcation zone. Guilt and recrimination echoed through her thoughts, reminding her that Katharine had wanted her to go home, had tried to get her to turn around; that her sister hadn't been able to get her to respond until she'd invoked the sacred safety lights and snapped Susan out of her self-absorbed desire to run wild and free. Under those thoughts was another, sharper and cleaner and oddly kinder, reminding her that their house, small and comfortable and familiar, where she kept all her things…well, that house was on the other side of the line. And depending on how far the desolation went, was very likely to have been wiped away along with everything else she'd seen there. Katharine wouldn't have wanted her to die. Katharine would have wanted her to finally be free.

If Katharine had just waited a few more seconds before invoking the safety lights, they could both have gotten away.

Susan pedaled on until a new thought struck her and she lost control of the bike, dumping herself onto the ground for the second time in a day. She was going the same direction the creature had gone. She curled herself into a ball, hugging her knees to her chest as the weight of the day crashed down over her, hitting harder than the ground. She had nowhere to go. Either she could enter a blasted wasteland that had stolen her sister—maybe her entire family—or follow the footsteps of a thing that couldn't possibly exist. There were no good choices left.

She stayed there, sobbing and shaking, for almost two hours before she was found by the search and rescue teams following the creature's trail of destruction back to its point of origin. They picked her up, cleaned her off, gave her orange juice and cookies and a warm place to sit in the back of an ambulance, and told her to stay put while they found her parents.

They never did.

Susan stayed put.

CHAPTER 4: AFTERMATH

4.1.

"Dr. Black?"

Susan looked up from the tablet where she'd been recording her observations of the latest tissue sample, frowning at the graduate student who had dared to interrupt her before she signaled her readiness to consider outside viewpoints. He was new to her lab: while she recognized him, she couldn't for the life of her remember his name.

That was fine. Based on what she'd seen so far, it wasn't as if he was going to be with them for long. Most graduate students got into "rift physics"—the casual name for the study of the quantum, spatial, and temporal distortions caused by the incursions—because they wanted action and excitement, not because they wanted to spend their lives squinting at complicated radiation scans, studying slides, or risking the loss of their senses after spending too much time looking at impossible colors. The ones who stayed were usually the ones whose lives had been directly impacted by the rifts, and this particular student wasn't on that list.

She'd know. She made it a point to personally interview every applicant who'd been wounded in some way by the rifts, verifying both their stability and their motivation for applying to work with her team. She'd met too many vigilantes, would-be scientists who saw rift physics as their route to taking revenge on the cosmic glitch that had destroyed their lives. They were easy to recognize. Something about their eyes, especially the ones who'd experienced direct exposure.

Takes one to know one, after all.

"Yes?" she prompted, when he continued to stand there without speaking. "I don't have time to wait around for you to remember what you wanted to tell me. Go bother your advisor if you—"

"You have a standing flag on the Evanston zone."

Susan went cold. "Yes," she said, after a moment's pause. "I do."

"There's been motion recorded inside."

"What?" Susan snatched the tablet out of his hands, scanning the grainy image on the screen for anything that looked different than it had the last thousand times she'd looked at the same scene.

Like all the exclusion zones, it hadn't visibly changed since it was formed. When the rifts opened from whatever unknown, presumably unknowable, dimension the creatures they belched forth originally inhabited, they brought a sphere of their own physical reality with them. It replaced and overwrote everything within it. She'd been told over and over again by the people who'd taken custody of her after the incident that she should consider herself fortunate; the Evanston zone was less than a quarter the size of the Chicago zone, which had swallowed three square miles of previously safe city. She had never once considered herself fortunate. That small exclusion zone had swallowed her sister, her childhood home, her hamster, and her parents, and if she missed the things she'd lost in that order, well, orphans of the incursion were allowed to be traumatized. People had given up on telling her that she had to be sad her parents were gone after the first year, two years before she'd stopped trying to sneak into the exclusion zone, even though she knew that no one had yet crossed the boundary line and lived.

Ten years before the first people had come out of the Manhattan exclusion zone.

4.2.

THE EXCLUSION ZONES warped and overwrote everything inside them with reality as it existed on the other side of the rift. The crackling coronas that surrounded the creatures when they first emerged had been envelopes of their native physics, which explained how they had been able to stand up under their own weight without pulverizing their bones, explained how they had been able to walk without shredding their muscles into paste. They walked into our world like they belonged here, and they walked *through* our world like they belonged here, and when they died, the envelopes of distortion fell with them, sinking into the ground they bled on.

Other than plummeting property values, it wasn't immediately clear what those little strips of modified physics had done. The bodies of the creatures had been confiscated and toted away for the sake of further research—one of the few times when every government in the world could be shown to act in apparent, if coincidental, tandem—and life had cautiously gone on. People whose homes hadn't been smashed or swallowed by the exclusion zones couldn't necessarily afford to move just because they were afraid of another monster stomping into their backyards; the phrase "once in a lifetime" was nowhere near large enough to describe what had just happened to them.

And at first, it had seemed like everything was fine, like life was getting back to normal, or as close to "back to normal" as it possibly could after an unspeakable, unprecedented event that had caused billions of dollars of property damage globally, and left countless people dead. It would have been bad enough if it *hadn't* occurred in the immediate aftermath of a global pandemic, when the world was still reeling, still frantically trying to piece their sense of normalcy back together.

Several churches decried the incursion as judgment day. Not everyone disagreed. Several splinter groups, already steeped in conspiracy and insular thinking after the long lockdown, insisted there had been no incursion: it had all been a Hollywood stunt, special effects and controlled explosions, intended to cover up the largest act of human trafficking in history. They were, thankfully, largely ignored, and returned to more ordinary conspiracies in the absence of true believers to support their latest fever dream.

Time passed. Families returned to their homes, not realizing they were now living within those invisible, intangible envelopes of changed space, and more time passed.

Babies were conceived, gestated, and born.

Some of the envelopes covered hospitals, meaning babies exited their mother's womb into a space where the laws of physics didn't work precisely as they worked in the "real" world as it was known and understood before. Those babies grew older, grew taller, grew stronger. And then, six years after the incursion, six years after the last rift had closed, while Susan was still pursuing her master's degree, still struggling to force science to give her the tools that would allow her to learn, once and for all, what had happened to her sister, those babies began to break the commonly understood laws of physics.

Some of them could lift cars over their heads with ease. Some of them could turn invisible. Some of them could move things with their minds.

Some of them could fly.

It took an almost embarrassingly long time for anyone to figure out that the common denominator of all these "super-children" was their location, both during gestation and birth. After that, it didn't seem to matter; a child who had been conceived, gestated, and born elsewhere and carried into one of the invisible fields of modified probability would no more evince such talents than a child born inside the field would lose them once removed from it.

(It would take several more years, and a research project organized by Susan herself, along with several of her fellow graduate students, before anyone confirmed that it was not just proximity to the fields, but the strength of the individual fields and the length of time an infant was gestated inside one or more of them, that determined that child's likelihood both of developing those talents, and the strength of the talents once developed.)

Maps were drawn, showing the places where it was safe to live and raise a family, the places where pregnant women shouldn't go, and the places where no one should go under any circumstances. In America at least, the government began acquiring as much of the land inside the fields as they possibly could, invoking eminent domain when money wouldn't expedite the process, and bit by bit, each exclusion zone developed a nearby tether of government properties, hopefully preventing more physics-defying individuals from entering the general population.

Sometimes Susan wished she'd been just slightly slower in her studies, so she could have pivoted to focusing on the children of the incursion, the ones whose lives would, through no fault of their own, never be normal. She couldn't fly or bend steel with her thoughts, but she still felt a strong kinship with those scared, confused superhumans, most of whom had been quickly surrendered to the state and moved into special schools where they couldn't tear cars in two unsupervised. The next arms race would be won by whoever could get their country's children into fighting shape the fastest, and once that became clear, it also became clear that this wasn't ushering in an era of superheroes and colorful capes filling the sky, but new and terrible means of waging war.

Recreating the rifts became the top priority of every government, and Susan found herself with a research contract the second she graduated. The people in charge of assigning funding believed that her close personal connection to the Evanston incident would keep her from getting distracted from her goal, and that her own loss would focus her energy on finding a way to break apart the fields that had taken her family.

And that whole time, inside the exclusion zone that had swallowed her sister, nothing moved.

Susan had spent the first three years after the incident running away from her grandparents, trying to slip past the military brigade and into the exclusion zone, intending to somehow find and recover her sister, never quite forgiving herself for her inability to step over the line.

She had spent the three years after *that* finishing high school, applying to colleges ("a rift opened in front of me and swallowed my sister" turned out to be exactly the kind of hook some people would kill for when it came time to compose her personal essays and convince the admissions committees to let her walk the hallowed halls of some of the finest institutions in the world) and preparing to find a bigger, better way of sneaking into the exclusion zone. She'd carried glorious dreams of coming up with a way to walk safely into the blasted lands, where the air was sometimes breathable and sometimes almost a living thing in the way it twisted in the throat, stealing breath away, where even the light could turn deadly in the blinking of an eye, to stride between the implausible dangers therein and find Katharine, miraculously unharmed, cowering in the shadow of some twisted building, ready to be rescued. Ready to come *home*.

The year after that, the first of the afflicted children was identified, and Susan, with her meticulous approach to documentation and statistics, had immediately requested and received permission to organize the mapping project that would verify their source, if not the reason for their communal strangeness. She had finished the project with her degree in one hand, graduation expedited by the pressing need for people in her new and rapidly evolving field of physics, and a job offer from the government waiting in the other hand.

She'd been in the first year of her tenure at her first lab when the news came echoing through the field of incursion physics like a shockwave, knocking down anything and everything in its path: two people had emerged from the Manhattan exclusion zone. It was one of the largest in the world, one of the strangest when seen from the outside, one of the deadliest when entered, and everyone who had been inside when the rift opened had long since been declared legally dead. There was no possible way anyone could have come out, but come out they had, hand in hand, dirty and scuffed and wearing clothing that had been mended and patched at least a dozen times, in some places with unfamiliar animal skins, the man holding a spear made from the hammered, reshaped bumper of a car, the woman carrying a machete. They had stopped when they reached the government blockade, standing in patient silence as they were swarmed by bewildered soldiers who didn't know what to do with this impossibility.

Someone must have known who fired first. Guns could be tested, after all; it was possible to know which one had been discharged. But the government never identified the soldier in question, and whoever it was, they were not disciplined in any way.

Things might have gone differently had the man not dropped the woman's hand and caught the bullet in his bare palm, looking at it for a long, disgusted moment before he tossed it idly aside.

"One of your research teams was found testing our boundaries last week," he said. "We don't want you here."

"We've been sent to make sure you understand that," said the woman. "This place is not for you. It wasn't for us, either, but it's ours now, and we refuse to surrender it to the world we left behind."

"Any further attempts to try our boundaries will be met with violence," said the man. He retook the woman's hand, and they turned and walked back into the inclusion zone without another word.

The next two years had seen a near-total stop in research into the incursion zones, until the first of the impossible children had demonstrated truly inexplicable abilities and the government had found a new direction for their focus. These children, unlike the populations of the exclusion zones, could be reached, could be acquired, could be studied. They were still a part of the world.

Twelve years after the incursion, Susan Black was settled in the second of her government-funded research labs, free from the need to worry about the outside world, free from the need to explain herself or justify her obsessions, legally permitted to access as much footage from the Evanston exclusion zone as her heart desired.

And she desired it. She desired it all. The next two years passed in a haze of analysis, late nights spent doing nothing but staring at the video they'd been able to capture from the safe side of the Evanston exclusion zone, making note of every gust of wind that carried anything over the line in either direction (leaves and debris blowing in from the "normal" side had a tendency to burst into flame within seconds, while the same coming from the exclusion side dissolved like sheets of ash, impossible to catch or keep), of every seagull foolish enough to glide over the demarcation.

(The seagulls kept flying, often rose even higher seemingly against their vague avian will—on the film, they often seemed to struggle, or to exhibit signs of confusion before flying intentionally back down to their lower starting points—and did not burst into flame, or explode, or any of the other changes that had been observed in less animate material. They did not, however, survive. So far, no seagull had been documented going more than a dozen or so yards past the line before it was snatched out of the air by forces either visible—long, whiplike tentacles that unfurled from the nearest "tree" and wrapped around it like cilia, dragging it downward in an explosion of feathers and gore that paled before the carnage that followed—or invisible, as the air itself seemed to wrap around the bird and squeeze. There was some correlation between which of the things happened; the "trees" seemed to feed about once a month when given the opportunity, whereas whatever controlled the wind was at once always ready for a kill, and oddly polite about waiting until all the "trees" had eaten before it took a gull.)

Susan's first formal project was an analysis of the time delay between living things entering the exclusion zone and their inevitable death. The government responded by releasing a hoard of small mammals near the border, most domestic, and using sound and light to frighten them over the line when they tried to run the other way.

Out of scientific dedication, Susan forced herself to watch the footage of the massacre that followed. She then wrote a sternly-worded letter to her superiors about how her work was explicitly not to be applied to living subjects, and any further such applications would result in her going into the private sector. She had already established herself as one of their most promising incursion researchers, and there had been no further animal trials, at least in part to placate her clearly unprofessional squeamishness.

Susan didn't care. As long as she never had to watch that sort of slaughter again, she was content to stay in her lab and continue to push the limits of what her equipment would allow.

Two years after that (seventeen years after the incursion), the first of the artificial rifts had been opened in her lab, using her equipment and her research. Three graduate students had been sucked through, screaming, never to be seen again. The entire building had been destabilized, and nothing had come out from the other side. But she could *do* it. She wrote politely sorrowful letters to the families of the presumably-deceased, she stood in front of the review committee convened to determine whether she had cut any corners or ignored any safety protocols—they found nothing; no one was as meticulous about safety protocols as Susan Black, the woman who seemed to view safety as a religion—or intentionally risked her team. And when they found her innocent of all wrongdoing, save, perhaps, for pursuing the unwise and unsafe science they had employed her to pursue, they published her findings, and settled her in her third posting.

This one was the closest to Evanston of any of her other facilities, located in Chicago, if well away from the exclusion zone. The logic was that proximity to the field might ease her way toward opening more stable rifts, and to make it even easier, the lab was located directly in the outline formed by the Chicago creature's body when it fell.

Susan wasn't sure she would have been able to work in the outline of the Evanston creature's body. She had always felt an odd kinship for that one, which had appeared in the moment she lost her sister, and which had brutally and inevitably died at the talons of its larger kin before the Chicago creature was gunned down by the United States army. She hadn't mourned for it, then or later, but she still would have felt like she was dancing on its grave if she had tried to work there.

In fifteen years of work and study and research, there had never been any sign of movement within the Evanston exclusion zone that hadn't originated from the "normal" side of the line. Fifteen years of stillness. And now she was being told that something was moving in there?

She squinted at the video, waiting for any flicker of motion. There: something that looked like a hand, or perhaps a fused pseudopod, flashed through the edge of the camera's view. They had tried, but had never been able to achieve a complete view of the zone's exterior. There were always dead spots, cameras that shorted out for no apparent reason, others that were somehow smashed without recording the means of their own destruction. Whoever belonged to the hand had either gotten very lucky, or knew exactly where the dead spots were.

It placed something atop a crumbled bit of masonry, pulling quickly out of the frame.

The something—a small dome—remained. A few seconds passed.

The dome began to flash, cycling through light and dark. Susan gasped, nearly dropping the tablet before she shoved it back into the hands of the student. He gaped at her.

"Get me a chopper," she snapped.

"What are you—?"

"I'm going to the exclusion zone."

CHAPTER 9: EXCLUDED

9.1.

Susan's Jeep rolled to a stop ten feet from the line—the proscribed safe distance. Any closer and the vehicle electronics would begin to malfunction, possibly causing the entire engine to short out and stranding her until a rescue crew arrived. The Jeep was still moving slightly when Susan threw herself out the door and ran for the border line, dropping her pack on the ground next to the wheel.

She stopped short of crossing over, the memory of the filmed massacre all too vivid in her memory. She wasn't a guinea pig or a rabbit—or, God forbid, a puppy—to be burst and torn apart by a gust of wind, but the military had sent scouts over the line again and again over the years, and size didn't seem to matter to whatever force it was that maintained the border. She wasn't going to risk it.

Their route had been designed to bring them to the camera that had captured the motion the night before. Susan squinted at the twisted landscape beyond the line. Even the sky was different. It wasn't possible. Nothing she'd seen since the storm rolled in to presage the rift had been possible; the last seventeen years of her life had been one long, layered impossibility.

And there, atop what had once been part of the cemetery wall, was the small dome she had seen put into place. It wasn't flashing anymore, but she recognized it all the same.

A safety light.

Sudden wild need gripped her. Susan took three long steps forward, almost touching the line, and cupped her hands around her mouth, shrieking as loudly as she could. "Katharine! Katharine! *Kitty!*"

It wasn't the first time she had come to the border and yelled for her sister. It was the first time in a long, long time when she had felt as if it might do something, and so when she lowered her hands, once again filled with the crushing despair that had become her constant companion over the intervening years, it was to turn away. So it was a safety light. So what. Something living on the other side of the line had probably found it in a junk heap or…or whatever they had over there (despite being one of the world's preeminent researchers into the exclusion zones, the lack of anything beyond what could be observed from the line meant that she was still as shockingly ignorant as anyone else) and decided to set it out somewhere. It was a coincidence. Not a sign.

Not a sign at all. She turned away, shoulders slumped. She was chasing a ghost. It was only fitting that they had lost each other in a cemetery, because she was chasing a ghost, and she was never going to see her sister again.

"Susie," said a voice behind her, rough and gravelly from disuse. Susan froze. "You're not going to believe it's me until you look at me, and I can't stay long. Come on, look."

Susan whirled, clapping her hands over her mouth, and looked at her sister for the first time in seventeen years.

Her first, irrational thought was that Katharine looked impossibly good for having spent the last decade and a half in a blasted hellscape where physics worked differently. She was tall—taller than Susan, anyway, by almost a foot—and her hair, while snarled, was still long and dark brown, streaked with gray at the temples. A long, twisting scar ran down one side of her face, slightly puckered where it had failed to heal perfectly, tugging the left corner of her mouth upward. She had no freckles. The sun on that side of the barrier must not work quite the same way.

Her clothes, visibly mended, were a patchwork of denim and knit, fabrics that could have been scavenged from any houses that stood through the descent of the exclusion zone.

"*Kitty*," Susan breathed, taking a step forward. Katharine held her hands up to stop her. They were swaddled in long strips of fabric that looked like they'd been cut from a sheet, little pink flowers on grimy white, and they explained the illusion of melted-together flesh that had appeared on the camera.

"Stop there," she said. "You can't come any closer. It's not safe."

"But Kitty," said Susan, aware that she was whining, unable to find the strength to stop. "Kitty, you're *right there*. You sent me a message, and I got it. I came."

"I sent the message because your soldiers don't think there's anyone on this side of the line to hear them," said Katharine, mouth twisting into a heart-achingly familiar moue of dismissive judgment. She didn't think much of the intelligence of the soldiers stationed to monitor the exclusion zone. "They mentioned you by name the last time a pigeon flew in here. Said you'd be fascinated by the data. So I knew you were nearby."

"I thought you were *dead!*" wailed Susan, voice breaking, voice traveling back in time seventeen years, to a time when it had been two teenage girls against the entire rest of the world, sisters with no support save for each other. Then a rift had opened between them, an actual physical rift, rather than the metaphorical ones they had seen separate other siblings, and they had each been somehow cast in what should have been the starring role of the other's life: anyone who knew the girls before the incursion would have tagged Katharine to become the borderline-obsessed government scientist with the sensible shoes and the memorized rule book, and Susan to become the grizzled survivor of an apocalyptic landscape, but that hadn't been the world's intention. Katharine stared at Susan, expression empathetic and longing, but didn't move toward her. Didn't even twitch.

Susan glared. "I thought you were *dead*," she repeated, more quietly. "The rift opened, and when it went away, everything on the other side was different, and you were gone, and I yelled and yelled, but you never came. I came back again and again, and I yelled and yelled, and you never came. Now you tell me you've been alive in here this whole time, and you won't even come over here and hug me?"

"I can't," said Katharine, not entirely apologetically. "The line protects me as much as it protects you."

"What are you even—"

"I would *die*, Susie. I barely survived the first time. It's too late for us. But it's not too late for my kids. Please, Susie. I need your help."

9.2.

THE SISTERS STARED at each other across a gulf of feet and worlds, and Susan couldn't find the words she needed to tell Katharine what she felt. How hard her heart was beating, how tight her skin was, how every neuron was firing at the same time, pain and pleasure intermingled and almost unendurable. She felt like she was on the verge of exploding, on the verge of catching fire, unsustainable.

"What…what happened?" she asked.

Katharine took a deep breath and turned her face away.

"When the aurora flashed down between us, I fell," she said. "The ground shook, and everything started to twist out of true, and I blacked out while the sky turned a thousand colors I'd never seen before. They hurt my head. It was like trying to think in math that didn't exist. When I woke up, the aurora was gone."

"Aurora?"

"The sheet of weird colors that flashed up along the barrier," said Katharine. "I could see you on the other side, but it was like looking through a piece of warped glass. You were all distorted and twisted in yourself, like you were some kind of monster. Through the colors, you were terrible. I would have run, but I had already fallen down."

Susan bit her lip. They had video recordings of the impossible colors in the rifts, of course, and they had managed their small, artificial tears in reality, but they had never been able to fabricate any sort of curtain that could actually be looked through. The distortion effect must have been a visual artifact of the human mind trying to process sensory input it wasn't supposed to have, turning it into something comprehensible at the expense of everything around it…Susan wrenched herself away from that train of thought, which threatened to drag her down more familiar pathways, picking at the possible ramifications of some new piece of data, and not focusing on the here and now, where she belonged.

"Could you hear me?"

"Not while the aurora was intact, and by the time I woke up the first time, you were gone. So were the colors. Instead, there was this…haze, clear and black at the same time, like specks of coal dust suspended in the air. It wasn't smoke, exactly, and it didn't move or spread, just hung there, throwing a veil between me and the rest of the world. I passed out again."

Susan frowned. "I was still in the same place when the rift closed. You weren't there anymore. There was no one there."

"Maybe time runs differently on the two sides of the divide, or maybe it did back then, and it's wound down a little since. Everything in here that isn't the way I remember the world being has been running down for the last couple of years."

That was news to Susan. Her frown deepened. "We haven't found any signs that the exclusion zones were breaking down."

"From the *outside*." Katharine looked at her knowingly. "From the outside, our family looked completely normal, didn't it? No one thought anything was wrong. But we were breaking down."

"True," Susan admitted. They had never really discussed it in solid detail, hadn't made anything as gauche as an actual plan, but they had both been silently aware that Katharine would be eighteen soon, and once she was, their parents would have no legal obligation to feed or house her. She'd been looking at colleges, focusing on ones that got good reviews from single parents attending for their degrees, and their shared intention had always been that Susan would go with her. They'd been willing to fight their parents for custody if necessary, and neither of them had anticipated much of a fight. Their parents had liked children so much more in theory than they ever seemed to in actuality.

"Sometimes you have to be inside a thing to understand it," said Katharine. She sounded sad. Susan was struck with a sudden, unexpected bolt of jealousy aimed at her older sister, who had been given the opportunity to understand Susan's life's work in a way that Susan herself never would.

But she wouldn't even have chosen this life if not for losing Katharine. This was *Katharine's* life, scientific and precise and regimented, not her own, wilder dream. If not for the rifts, Susan would have chosen the horizon over the known hazards of home. Her jealousy was misaimed. No matter what Katharine had been able to experience on her side of the line, her future had been stolen from her and given to Susan, who had no right to resent the life her sister had gotten in its place that Susan didn't get to understand.

It still stung.

"Why didn't you come out?" she asked. "I've seen things go through. I know the line is permeable. I know you could have come out."

"I couldn't though." Katharine cocked her head. "Not at first. The black specks in the air wouldn't let anyone leave, and when people tried, they ripped them apart. There weren't that many of us left, even in the beginning."

"Mom and Dad...?"

"Dead before I found them," said Katharine. "Their house… it *folded*, like a piece of paper, like something was trying to make an origami crane or something, and they were inside when it happened, they never had time to run. I found them, or what was left of them, anyway, when I woke up and finally went looking."

"Oh."

Susan had accepted the fact that her parents were probably dead long before she'd accepted the same about her sister. It had been a much less painful process. They were people who shared her genes (but less so than her sister; each of them was half of her, but Kitty was the whole of her, one hundred percent drawn from the same genetic stew, and it was only natural her loyalty should tilt toward her only sibling, and not toward the parents who had made them almost casually, as if they were the byproducts of a recipe they were just trying out, but not entirely sure they wanted to commit to).

She'd consoled her grandparents when they came down from Wisconsin to collect their sole remaining grandchild, and had been clear-headed enough even at the time to talk them into relocating to Chicago, arguing that property costs would never be lower (and indeed, they had rebounded within five years, more than quadrupling the value of their home), but she had never mourned her parents. Not the way she'd mourned her sister.

Not the way she was still mourning her sister, even now that she was standing only a few feet away from her, looking at the details of her familiar, unfamiliar face.

It would have been worse in a time before social media. There was a period where losing the family home would have meant losing every trace of Katharine, every picture that wasn't stiff and posed and deemed appropriate for the extended family, every recording of her voice. But Susan's phone had survived the storm, and it kept pieces of her sister with her, even after all this time.

"Can I tell the story now? Or are you going to keep asking questions?"

"I can be quiet while you explain things, but I'm going to have questions when you're finished."

The corner of Katharine's mouth twisted wryly. "I'd be surprised if you didn't."

"So please." Susan spread her hands. "Tell me how you survived. And then tell me why you called me here."

9.3.

"I WILL, BUT before I go any further, I need you to take out your phone and any other electronics you have on you and toss them to me."

"What? Why?"

"Because there are some things I don't want your people listening to me say."

Susan thought about why that could be, and landed on, "Kitty, if you had to…do things in there in order to survive, they would understand. *I* would understand. I would never judge you. Please trust me that far."

"I do, but I need you to trust me too." They stared at each other, and Susan knew she was going to give in, because this was her first and maybe only time seeing her sister again, even before the next thing Katharine said. "*Please*, Susan."

"All right." Susan took out her phone (new, government-issued, not personal; her personal phone, with its treasure trove of pictures, was safely back at her apartment) and threw it through the barrier, followed by her tablet. At least everything up until this point had been recorded and stored in the cloud, and she knew all the drones and recorders sent into the zone shorted out as soon as they passed the barrier; remote-control robots no more complex than those sold in toy stores died just as quickly, and the ones simple enough to keep going would be snatched and smashed apart by the trees. She wasn't worried about Katharine's people getting their hands on any proprietary data.

"Thank you," her sister said.

"*Now* will you finish telling me the story?"

"The last time I saw you, you were starting to pedal toward me after I called safety lights. The sky was green as Oz, and I just *knew* a tornado was about to hit right on top of us. I wanted you to move faster. I wanted you to trust me. I wanted—God—I wanted us to face the storm together. And then the aurora happened. It was like someone ripped the air in half and turned it into a sheet of solid carnival glass filled with those impossible colors. I could still see you, but at the same time, you weren't you. You were this horrible, distorted, monstrous *thing*. Maybe that was the only moment where I could have gotten out. I don't know. I just know it was the only time where there was much of a concerted effort to keeping us from running at the line.

"The colors hurt. Looking at them *hurt*. It's the only way I can explain what it was like, like trying to do math too big for your brain or sing along with music humans aren't supposed to hear. I'd already fallen off my bike, and I think I whacked my head on the concrete when that happened, because I passed out. I don't know how long I was unconscious. Long enough to miss the aurora going away, and save myself."

"Save...?" Susan caught herself before the question could finish forming, but she couldn't stop herself from starting to ask. She bit her lip, feeling like a teenager again as Katharine looked at her in silent amusement.

"We got further than I thought we would before you had to interrupt," said Katharine. "When the aurora went away, it took everyone who was looking at it with it. Not right away for most of them—I mean, yeah, some of them had brain aneurysms and died on the spot. The rest got to live for a few weeks while their eyes melted out of their skulls and their minds refused to process what they'd seen. Remember that old story about the color that drove men mad?"

"H.P. Lovecraft was a racist prick," said Susan, almost automatically.

"Yeah, he was, but he was a racist prick who wrote a story that entered the cultural consciousness, which makes him a *useful* racist prick right now," said Katharine. "A tool's a tool. Sometimes you use what you have, instead of wasting energy on throwing it away and starting over from scratch. May I continue?"

"Hey, you asked *me* if I remembered the story," protested Susan. "I remember it. It was called 'The Color Out of Space.' They made movies. None of them were any good."

"Huh," said Katharine, sounding a little pleased by the news of Lovecraft's cinematic failure. "Well, this was like that. If you looked at the aurora for too long—and a lot of people did—you never stopped seeing it, not even after it went away, and that would eventually kill you. Either it would bake your brain or your eyes, and whichever it was, it always ended the same way. If I hadn't fallen off my bike when I did, I'd be dead too, and we wouldn't be having this conversation."

Susan didn't say anything, thinking about the researchers who'd given their professional lives and sometimes their sanity chasing the colors of the rift. None of them had died by any means other than suicide—at least not as far as she was aware—but none of them had been documented having that kind of sustained direct contact. On her side of the exclusion line, the colors had only appeared inside an active rift, not everywhere in the sky, and of all the people on record, she was the one who'd been closest to an open rift the longest.

If anyone else had been closer, they hadn't been found, or hadn't come forth, or hadn't survived. The possibilities were endless, and suddenly, none of them seemed even remotely positive.

"After the aurora faded and before the deaths began, I picked myself up from the ground and you were gone. The last thing I'd seen of you, you'd been a monster, so maybe it was a good thing that you weren't there for me to find, but I couldn't think that way. Everything on my side of the line was blasted, like we'd been hit by some sort of nuclear explosion, but if that had been what happened, I wouldn't have woken up at all. No one stands at ground zero of a nuke and survives to go looking for their baby sister." Katharine's mouth twisted. "On your side of the line, the grass was green, and the pavement was intact. It was like...like the world was a bad CGI landscape, and someone had patched in something from the wrong program. My side of the line was bad code. Your side of the line was ordinary.

"It took me a long time to decide it was safe to try stepping over. I had to consider the pros and cons, and you were gone and I didn't have all the information and what I did have was impossible. Everything was burning. The trees looked like they were *breathing*. The buildings I could see were all bent up and twisted and wrong, and I didn't know what to do, and that indecision saved my life. I was spared because I was too scared to go charging straight ahead. You remember Chuck Weatherby?"

Susan blinked. Chuck had lived three doors down from them when they were kids. "Yeah," she agreed.

"He wasn't in the cemetery when the aurora dropped, but he was close enough to see where it ended, and he'd been making his way toward the border since the split. His parents weren't home when it happened. He was trying to get back to them. I was about to walk toward the line when he came charging past me. Knocked me over, he was in such a hurry." Katharine shook her head.

"So there I am, on the ground for the third time in one day. I shouted after Chuck, tried to get him to slow down, tried to make him turn around and see me—he'd knocked me over, he could damn well *see* me—and then I stopped, because if we were both alive and the trees were breathing, who knew what else was in here with us? I was still thinking like I was going to get out of here, you see. It would take a while before we adapted our thinking to our situation. Anyway, Chuck ran for the line, and I watched him go, and when he got there, he charged right into the black stuff hanging in the air. Just right into it, like it didn't even matter. Like he didn't even see it—and maybe he didn't. Maybe he was so scared and eager to get back to something that looked like normal that he didn't slow down enough to see what he was running through."

Katharine's face twisted, disgust and sorrow warring for ownership of her expression. "He ran *into* it. He didn't run *out* of it. It was only about two feet across, even back then. He should have been able to pass through it in one long step, especially at the speed he was going. And instead, he slowed down, like he was moving in slow-motion, like the black stuff was pushing against him, and then he…came apart."

Susan, who had reviewed every scrap of footage from every exclusion zone in the world, had never seen anything like what her sister was describing. She stared.

"I know how it sounds. I *know*. But it's true. He came apart into this fine red mist, and the black stuff drank it down, and I knew I wouldn't be getting out of here any time soon. The black stuff—the membrane—gets thinner every year. Nothing could get through it at all for the first year, and then birds and bugs and squirrels started coming through. We've even seen a few cats and stray dogs, although not for long. Either something gets them, or they get sick from trying to breathe in here."

"But you're breathing just fine," Susan protested.

"Yeah. Whatever the change did to the atmosphere, it doesn't seem to bother people. Or maybe it bothers us in a way we don't have the technology in here to understand. What I wouldn't give for even the equipment that comes with a mobile clinic..." Katharine's expression turned distant, like she was lost in a sweet fantasy of X-rays and portable diagnostic units. It only lasted a moment before she was continuing: "If you made it through the first few days, you're fine. Better than fine. We have no airborne diseases. Nothing communicable at all. With our population size, we should have at least a few sexually-transmitted diseases, at least one or two chronic medical conditions, and we don't. Everyone inside the barrier is just as healthy as a horse that can't get out of the pasture."

"We...we didn't know."

"Well, how could you? I don't know if this happened anywhere else, but this is the first time the council has agreed to let someone have direct contact with the outside world since the barrier thinned enough to make it possible for us."

"You have a governmental structure?"

"Susie. Really. That's what surprises you? We're *people*. People like to have at least some rules. They don't like oppression, but they like to know that if someone crosses the line, they'll be held accountable in some way. *Of course* we have a council. We don't have so many people in here that we can't usually find consensus, but we have enough that we don't want to live in anarchy, and we don't want to worry about being killed for the contents of our pockets every time we let our guards down."

"Oh," said Susan, feeling faintly ashamed of her assumptions.

"It took about a year before some of the bigger gangs that had formed after the shift decided to come together and form a provincial government. That's a long story—it's not important now—but they made rules, and we all agreed to them. It's not worth my freedom to fight those rules. It might have been, if the barrier had come down any faster. I wanted to get back to you more than I'd ever wanted anything in my life. I was so scared that you really were the monster I'd seen through the aurora, that the thing that twisted the land around me had twisted the people outside it. Maybe this was the safe side, despite everything we had to tell us it wasn't, and you were lost. And with every year that passed without the barrier letting us leave, it made more sense to stay, to listen to the council when they said we couldn't make contact with the world outside. I'm sorry, Susie. I stopped trying to find a way back to you after the first five years. I couldn't keep torturing myself with something I was never going to have, that probably wasn't even going to matter."

"I understand," said Susan numbly. She did and she didn't. Katharine had given up on her, but she had never given up on Katharine. She had whittled her life to the bone trying to reach across the divide and pull her sister home. "But you can leave now?"

"The barrier lets us through now," Katharine said. "We've had scouts probing the edge of the world for the last few years. I never went with them. I knew there…I knew there was nothing for me to find, and if there was, I didn't deserve it anymore. I stopped deserving it as soon as I gave up on getting out."

"Oh, *Kitty*." Susan sighed. "You said you didn't know if this had happened anywhere else? It did. It happened all over the world. It happened to *Chicago*. And what you call the aurora was a black dome from the outside."

"I knew it was a dome," said Katharine. "I could see the bend after the membrane started to thin. But…all over the world? Really?"

"Everywhere. We didn't see the colors outside, except where the world tore in what we called rifts, and monsters came out."

"Monsters."

"Giant Godzilla monsters. They came out of the rifts and they stomped away and when they found each other, they fought, and they killed each other, and we killed the rest of them, and they all died, and the rifts closed, and the domes popped, but we couldn't go over the line." Susan didn't mention that on her side, much of the reticence had been enforced by the government. It hadn't been that way everywhere: some countries had taken volunteers to try to cross, while others had been more than happy to "volunteer" people they viewed as political prisoners, or criminals, or otherwise unwanted members of their society. None of them had been able to pass. They hadn't come apart into red mist the way Kitty said Chuck Weatherby had, but they had all died on the spot.

Most of the bodies had fallen into the exclusion zone and been lost. The ones that had fallen on the safe side of the line had been retrieved and autopsied, confirming cause of death as a massive heart attack in every confirmed case. The bodies that hadn't been recovered had all disappeared within a day, in various horrific ways.

"We didn't see any monsters on this side," said Katharine. "Not at first, anyway. Whatever keeps us all from getting sick, it changed the plants and animals. I know your cameras have picked up on the trees feeding. They're not trees anymore. They *look* like trees, but if you cut a seed open, what's inside is more like a small anemone, and if you plant them, they grow looking just like their parents, branches, leaves, and all. It's some of the most sophisticated mimicry I've ever seen."

Susan didn't say anything, just blinked. It made sense that life inside the exclusion zone would have a mutative property, given what the fields did to children gestated inside them, but with no way to collect samples, that had only ever been a theory. "Monsters?"

"We had dogs at first. Now we have…we don't really have a name for them, because it's been impossible to reach a consensus. They still look like dogs, but if you touch them, you get stuck, and they gradually envelop and consume you. It's not a pretty death. You have time to suffer. It was worse in the beginning, when it was dogs we knew, who knew us, changing. You didn't get stuck every time back then. You could pet them if you were fast and your hands were clean and dry—moisture and dirt seem to speed the process. But that changed too, and we had to watch those dogs cry and mourn because they didn't understand why their people abandoned them."

"And cats?"

"Basically big mouths running from the base of the ribcage to what used to be the actual jaw, filled with teeth and venom. It was easier on the cats. Not on the cat people. Death by cat is a really nasty way to go." Katharine shuddered, a gesture that didn't look wholly exaggerated.

Susan hesitated but had to ask. "My hamster?"

To her surprise, Katharine laughed. "Oh, little sister. You sound more worried about that rodent than you did about our parents. I guess they did a number on us, huh? All the rodents spit poison now. It's acidic, and it can eat through steel. Your hamster never got the chance to develop the talent. The crush that destroyed our house killed the poor little guy. He didn't suffer."

Not like the people inside the exclusion zone. "But the people are still the same?"

"The ones who were trapped in here, yeah. We're too healthy, but we haven't turned into masses of tentacles wrapped in a semi-human skin. We just can't leave."

"Some people came out of the Manhattan exclusion zone about a decade ago."

"And has anyone else ever come out of any of the...what did you call them, 'exclusion zones'? Or were those the only ones?"

Susan was silent. There were rumors, of course, rumors that people had somehow been forcibly removed from the Shanghai or Moscow exclusion zones and held for further study, but they were just that: rumors. She had never seen any research that would indicate access to materials the rest of the world didn't have, and while America wasn't currently on good terms with either China or Russia, the global community of rift physicians had ways of passing things around. They needed to understand the conditions that had made the incursion possible, and the mechanism by which it had been able to deposit slivers of its own physics into Earth's previously immutable reality.

They needed to know how to send up the alarms if it was about to happen again. Everything else—national secrets, national security—was secondary to that goal.

Katharine nodded. "There you go. Is the Manhattan exclusion zone bigger than this one?"

"The zones seem to have formed based on the population density of the local urban centers," said Susan. "So the Chicago zone is bigger than the Evanston zone, and the Tokyo zone is the largest in the world."

Also the best-defended. The appearance of giant monsters and interspatial rifts had only confirmed what Japanese media had been telling the population was inevitable for decades, and the government had been forced to lock their national exclusion zones down like prisons to prevent the panic following the incursion from reaching cataclysmic levels. If anything ever came out of the exclusion zones, it wouldn't be coming out of Japan.

"So the Manhattan one must be pretty big," said Katharine thoughtfully. For a moment, Susan felt like she wasn't even necessary to the conversation. "All right, then, that fits with my observations. They must have felt things changing sooner than we did, and so they sent someone out to tell you to stay away, am I right?"

"Yes, but..."

"I told you that you can't come in. The barrier would let you pass at this point, but everything on this side of the line would see you as an intruder. The trees would wake up if they hadn't been fed recently, the dogs would come running toward the smell of you, the moles and voles that have managed to survive the burrowing beetles would come boiling out of the ground. Unless you masked yourself somehow, you'd die in minutes, and that would be the kinder option."

"So I can't come in. Why can't you come out?"

"I told you we hadn't changed in here, and that was mostly the truth, but only mostly. We still have all the same organs, in all the same places. They've just...shifted a little, to accommodate our new surroundings. The speed wouldn't make sense on the other side of the line—mature organisms don't mutate the way they have in here—but everything seems to happen faster on this side of the barrier. We have some doctors who were caught when everything came down. They've done autopsies, and they've charted the changes."

Susan was almost embarrassed by the way the hair on her back of her neck stood up, her skin tightening with sudden, atavistic *wanting*. This was information no one in the world had—not the world as she knew it, anyway—and if she could get her hands on it, she could unlock some of the secrets of the modified children, the little superhumans who were being courted and claimed by governments the world over. "Do you have written notes of any kind?"

"Yes, and I have permission to offer to share them with you if that's what it takes to convince you to help us."

Katharine's words were flat and devoid of inflection. Susan winced. Her first time speaking to her sister in seventeen years and she was already treating her like a research subject. That wasn't how this was supposed to go; they should be embracing, laughing and clinging to each other, not standing on opposite sides of an almost-invisible line, a barrier that wasn't there anymore, talking calmly about exchanging research notes.

"Why *can't* you come out?" asked Susan, resisting the urge to stomp her foot. It was childish. She was looking at a woman she'd last known as a child, and it felt like she was sliding backward along the trail of her own life, years melting away, replaced by awkward strangeness. She wasn't a scientist anymore, wasn't a respected researcher for the United States government. She was a teenage girl who wanted nothing more in the world than to put her arms around her sister, press her face against her shoulder, and sob.

"Because our lungs don't work like yours do anymore," said Katharine. "The air in here is different. I'd ask you to send in an air quality meter, but nothing more complicated than alkaline batteries survives for long this side of the barrier. I don't know what we *are* adapted to breathe, but it's not the same mix you have out there."

"Can you re-adapt?"

"I don't think so. When we try to leave—and we know where the dead spots on your cameras are, we've been testing the boundary since it got thin enough to let us pass—we get about ten minutes before asphyxia sets in. Which is why I was able to get permission to contact you."

"You mentioned kids. When you said you needed my help."

"Yeah. You're an auntie." Katharine smiled, bright as she ever had. "Victor and Susan. I named her after you. They're perfect. I wish you could have met them before this. I think you'd have loved them."

"How can I help your kids if I can't cross the line?" Katharine had said that everyone inside was healthy, but maybe she'd been exaggerating; maybe she needed Susan to throw insulin or chemotherapy drugs through the barrier for her children's sake. Although it didn't make sense for both of them to be affected, or for Katharine to have come alone. Surely if she was trying to get help for sick children, she would have brought them with her, to look solemnly at the aunt they'd never met while their mother begged for their lives.

"The children are...different."

Susan didn't say anything.

Katharine looked at her, clearly desperate, just as clearly not sure what she could possibly say to make this all go the way she needed it to go. "Some people *can* pass the barrier and not get swarmed the second they step onto our ground. I don't know why. No one's ever been able to figure out what makes them different, but they *are* different. When we've seen them, there have been little auroras in the air around them, like part of the original barrier has attached itself to them. They can come and go, and they absolutely do, even when we ask them not to. We've killed a few of them."

Susan thought about what she knew, and everything she'd theorized, and said, very slowly and carefully, "When the creatures came through the rift, they seemed to carry some of their reality with them. We've always assumed the exclusion zones were the consequence of that incursion, like shooting a bullet through a clay plate. You live in the distortion of the impact. I told you the creatures all died?"

Katharine nodded.

"Well, where the bodies fell, that...that thin layer of reality, whatever it was, sank into the ground and stayed behind. The rules of the universe don't work quite the same way inside those envelopes. Fires catch more quickly, things explode more easily, bugs have been getting bigger...it's like they've revoked parts of the square-cube law." Better not to mention the children. At least not yet.

To her surprise, Katharine looked relieved. "Have any children been born inside one of those 'envelopes' of different universal law?"

Susan nodded. "Yes, but it hasn't been long enough for them to grow up and become the people who've been bothering you."

"The children are important, too, but this is an experiment with a lot of different moving pieces, and they all matter. That's the problem with complex systems. You have to account for all the variables if you want them to hang together." She held up three fingers. "I have three theories to propose. All right?"

"Go ahead."

"Theory the first, people who have spent an excessive time inside one of those 'envelopes' may have picked up residual effects. Not as severe as restructured lungs, but little lingering impacts from the exposure."

"That would explain the auroras you saw when those people came through your barrier," Susan said. "If you're comfortable coming back to meet me tomorrow, I can bring a couple of our researchers who've spent long periods of time inside the envelopes, and see whether any of them have those auroras around them." Inwardly, she cursed at the unfairness of it all. Her own lab was located inside one of the impact zones. If anyone had been exposed long enough to be able to safely cross the barrier, it should have been her. But she had only been in this specific location for a short period, and she didn't live in her lab, didn't sleep there most nights. The amount of time needed was probably measured in years, which explained why they didn't have more people gallivanting across the barrier.

Katharine nodded. "Theory the second, children either conceived or born inside those 'envelopes' have exhibited unusual attributes or traits that are viewed as in some way desirable by the rest of the population."

Susan schooled her face, even as she nodded, and said, "That's less of a theory, more of a question. I don't know whether long exposure to the modified natural laws inside the impact zones would give people the ability to cross your barrier and enter an exclusion zone without being targeted by the exclusion zone's immune system. I do know that children born inside the outline of the impact have been documented exhibiting unusual capabilities."

Katharine paused. "I know we're on different sides right now—physically as well as metaphorically—but can we be blunt with each other?"

"Please," said Susan. The tension of talking to her older sister like they were spies for different factions of a war was getting to her.

"Do those kids have superpowers?"

CHAPTER 16: CAPES AND CHANGES

16.1.

For a moment, all Susan could do was stare at her sister, not quite sure how to deal with the scope of that question. Finally, she swallowed and straightened. "That's classified."

"Dammit, Susie, I thought we agreed no more bullshit."

"I threw my own recording devices away, but I don't control our surroundings, and there's a chance someone has a microphone close enough to pick us up. You're smart enough to have survived in there for seventeen years. You know all this."

"Fine," snapped Katharine. "Let's say, for the sake of argument, that some of those kids have superpowers. Something desirable, something world governments would like to get their hands onto. Something you can't replicate under the normal laws of physics. Hypothetically."

"We can hypothetically say that," Susan agreed.

"Let's also say that it's common enough that if the whole world doesn't know for sure, people are gossiping about it, and there are lots of rumors out there in the air." Katharine fixed her with a hard look. "Let's also say that if my baby sister is too concerned about her employers hearing her say something naughty to confirm this theory, that the government is probably also very invested in making those children disappear."

"That might be one possibility, but it confirms nothing," said Susan. "I might also add that *if* this were happening, it would make sense for it to be happening all over the world."

"A biological arms race," said Katharine. "Every government would want to have more kids with inexplicable abilities in *their* custody, working for *them*. So they'd be acquiring them as fast as they could, hopefully before another government with more guns showed up to take their new toys away."

Susan said nothing.

"So it would also follow that people who *aren't* part of the government—criminals, capitalists, people who wanted to work just a little outside the lines—would be looking to acquire some of those children for their own purposes." Katharine shook her head, mouth pressed into a hard line. "It would be the only thing that made sense. No one wants to be left with the rock when everybody else has a machine gun."

"Yes," said Susan carefully. "Which all leads you to what conclusion?"

"Someone—multiple someones if we're not the largest or most appealing of your exclusion zones—realized people who'd been in one of those impact spots for long enough could come and go inside the exclusion zones as they pleased. And oh, they pleased."

Susan looked at her blankly. Katharine sighed.

"We use things in here. We're very, very skilled recyclers. But we don't *need* everything that has value out on your side of the border. Diamonds? Old tech we haven't been able to use since the power cut out? Pretty much any sort of antique you can come up with that doesn't have an immediate practical application? Hell, even *money*. Without putting the kids into the equation at all, there's so much in here that could have value to your world and means nothing to ours."

"So why not set up trade with our world? I'm sure you're low on…on chocolate and salt and cooking wine by now. We could give you the things you can't make on your own."

"And would your government be happy to let us keep taking care of ourselves? Making our laws, doing things our own way? We can't communicate between exclusion zones. I don't know if our methods are standard or if they're oddly harmonious or somewhere in the middle. Maybe this is hell and the Chicago zone is utopia. We're only a few miles apart, but we don't have any way to go over there and check, and we can't leave. Right now, part of what's keeping the United States Army from rolling through the barrier is that they can't be sure what will happen if they do, and that means their lack of knowledge is one of the strongest protections we have. So no. It was hard enough to get the council to agree to even let me signal you."

This was already the longest conversation anyone had had with someone inside an exclusion zone since the incursion. Susan was going to be up all night taking readings on herself, blood and tissue samples, to make sure her proximity to the barrier hadn't negatively impacted her. She both desperately wanted to be able to help her sister, to be trustworthy and deserving of this long, unique encounter, and for the government to somehow still be recording every syllable and every pause so she could replay it over and over again, forever. This was an incredible research opportunity, and she was frittering it away.

Frittering it away on being a human being for a change. She quashed the part of her that wanted to steer the conversation back to life inside the exclusion zone—how the last seventeen years had passed, how they had survived, how Katharine, her beloved, rule-following sister, had been able to adapt and even thrive in a totally transformed world—and said, instead, "That means this was really important. What do you need?"

"My *children*," said Katharine, with sudden desperation. Her expression of calm resolve cracked, and for a moment, Susan saw her sister for what she really was: a desperate mother trying to save her family through the only channel she had left. A narrow channel, not entirely trustworthy, but still open. Still worth trying.

"What happened?"

Katharine took a deep breath.

16.2.

"TWO DAYS AGO. A group of men came through the barrier from your side. They were dressed all in black, and carrying machetes as long as my arm. Not knives—machetes. They must have already known guns didn't work in here, and there's no reason to sneak into someone's backyard under cover of darkness with a machete in your hand unless you're planning to cause trouble. There were five of them. Three were wearing masks. The other two had goggles. They wanted to make sure that if they were caught on camera, they couldn't be identified."

Susan made a small sound of understanding, already intending to have all the nearby surveillance footage pulled and gone over with a fine-toothed comb. A group of armed men must have set off a red flag *somewhere*.

"They made it past our sentries and into the center of the city. We were careless." The admission was made bluntly, with a more than reasonable amount of self-loathing. "We forgot that just because nothing had happened, that didn't mean things couldn't start happening again, and we got complacent. They made it right into our homes. And they went straight for the children."

Implying this had been in the works for some time, and more, that the people responsible had some method of surveilling the exclusion zones. The thought of someone else being able to observe an entirely new, not entirely human society while she couldn't burned. Her jealousy was so strong it was almost a physical pain in her chest. "How many?"

"How many what?"

"Children, Kitty. How many children did they take?"

"Four." Katharine took a shaking breath. "My two and two others. They grabbed them and ran. We went after them, but they had a head start and they must have knocked the kids out somehow, there's no other way they could have taken them all. But they have to know what our kids can do. They have to be planning to use them, or sell them. I don't know. I just know that we're scared and we need help. Please, Susie. I know it's been a long time, but please. Save our kids."

Susan nodded, taking a step back. "I'll do my best," she said.

16.3.

AFTER SUSAN AGREED to help, she and Katharine worked out their signals if they needed to contact each other again, and Katharine promised to have the border watched for signs of Susan's return. Then they walked away, two sisters heading in opposite directions, this time intentionally.

The armed soldiers who had watched the whole encounter stepped back as Susan approached, making room for her to get back into her Jeep. She looked at her driver, face impassive. "Well?" she said. "Drive. Now."

There were no new observers in her lab, no new flags on her file: there was no way she could hide the fact that she'd had extended close contact with someone inside an exclusion zone, but they either hadn't been able to hear her conversation or were still reviewing the recording. Susan didn't care which as long as they weren't rescinding her clearance yet. She flung herself at her work station, snapping, "Pull all the video feeds from the area surrounding the Evanston zone, and do it *now*."

Did she have research access to any of the children currently in custody? She pulled up the relevant dashboard, and sighed with relief when she saw the confirmation that she did. She sent off a quick request for any recent electromagnetic scans. She knew they were taken daily as the children developed their abilities; hopefully comparing them to scans from people who had never been in a known impact zone, and to her own scans, when she knew she didn't have whatever "field" would have granted her safe passage, would tell her what she was looking for. If some of those children came from within exclusion zones, and if she could find something about their fields that she could scan for to identify other people with similar fields, then a detector to spot any radiation signatures that shouldn't be out among the general public could help her find these men. It was a lot of "ifs," but it was really all she had to go on.

Of course, a detector like that could also help her employers find all the children who had or might develop strange capabilities, but that was a problem for later. She kept typing, pulling up files and scanning them as quickly as she could. She had willingly sold herself to the government in her quest for funding and answers and even the slimmest chance that she would be able to help her sister. She had done this, all of this, for Katharine. She had shaped her entire life according to what Katharine needed, what *she* needed if she was going to have any chance at all of saving her sister.

But the whole time, her sister had been surviving just fine on her own. Not surviving: thriving. The version of Katharine who'd stood there self-assured and explaining what the exclusion zones had done to the animals around them. The comfortable, confident Katharine who had two children and kept them alive in a mutated wasteland…that wasn't a Katharine who would have been possible without the incursion. The monsters that had ended so many lives and ruined so many futures had made her sister's life and future possible.

What right did Susan have to take that away from her? What right did the United States government, who hadn't been able to find a way to get her out before the mutations meant she could never leave, have to tell her how to live? Susan had always hated how reluctant the government was to force their way past the barrier in the first days after the incursion, and that was when she'd thought she'd just be retrieving her sister's body, not her actual sister. Now, knowing what she did, she couldn't help hating them again, just a little.

One of the programs she had set to review the footage from the cameras surrounding the Evanston exclusion zone beeped softly, catching her attention, and Susan swiveled, switching her attention to the appropriate monitor.

There, four men dressed in black, with masks covering the lower halves of their faces, were climbing out of an unmarked white van. Susan swore silently. This would have been easier before the pandemics, when even people who were preparing to break the law would sometimes forget to pull their masks up while they were on camera. Or maybe she was just viewing the past through rose-tinted glasses again, as she had scolded so many students for doing.

"Dr. Black?"

Susan looked up and scowled. It was that grad student again. She was going to have to learn his name, if only so she could yell at him for disturbing her while she was trying to work. "*What?*" she demanded.

"Um. It's, uh, it's General Anderson. He wants to see you."

Susan sighed and stood. She'd known this was coming. That didn't make it less disruptive. "Thank you…"

"Oh. Um, Harris."

"Thank you, Harris." She paused. When he didn't say anything else, she prompted, "And he's waiting for me where, exactly?"

"Oh! I'm sorry. I wasn't expecting to see the general here today." He cleared his throat. "The lobby, Doctor."

"Please tell Karen to prepare the conference room," said Susan, and turned to walk briskly toward the door. Harris, blessedly, didn't follow.

The government taking over all incursion research and managing all rift physics funding meant that even though most of their employees were civilians, they had learned how to fall into a quasi-military structure. As civilian contractors, they weren't required to follow the divisions of rank all the time, or with nearly the compliance of the enlisted researchers, but disrespecting a ranking officer was a quick way to lose your position. And since the government controlled the field, if she lost this position, she'd never get another one.

She walked from the lab to the hall, and down it to the stairs. A quick descent later and she was approaching a small cluster of men in dress uniforms standing in a rough semi-circle in the middle of what had once been a hospital lobby. Like many modern rift physics centers, her lab had been built in a location that had existed before the incursion, sparing construction crews the need to spend any more time than absolutely necessary inside the envelope of distorted space.

Susan sometimes wondered whether the consideration was a union thing, or tied to the fact that the government tended to use their own people for construction, and didn't want to expose them more than they had to. They certainly didn't show the same consideration for the custodial or janitorial staff of the building.

"General," she said, as she drew close enough to be heard without shouting. "I understand you wanted to see me, sir."

"Ah, Dr. Black." He turned, smiling his patented fatherly smile at her. Susan smiled tightly back. She had managed, thus far, to keep him from realizing she was immune to fatherly concern and manipulation, and she wanted to keep it that way for as long as possible. "I heard you've had an exciting day."

I'm sure you did. "Yes, sir. I was able to make contact with a resident of the Evanston exclusion zone."

"Your sister, I believe."

"Yes, sir."

"How was this accomplished? None of your reports have indicated any success at getting communications into the zone." Because there hadn't been any: nothing had ever been found to work, not at any of the zones whose researchers shared their data with Susan's lab, which meant that save for a few less than friendly countries, she could say with some assurance that today had been the longest ever mutually initiated communication with a zone resident.

"When we were kids, we set up a pass to tell each other when things were really serious and we needed to pay attention," she said. "Safety lights."

"Safety lights," repeated the general, disbelievingly.

"Yes, sir. There was a movie, *Ghostbusters*, and one of the main characters said—"

"Safety lights are for dudes," finished the general, and raised an eyebrow. "I've seen a few movies in my day, Dr. Black. Did you and your sister have a poor opinion of the men in your lives?"

"All due respect, sir, we were teenagers. We had a poor opinion of every adult in the world. We established the code long before the incursion—obviously—and she had reason to believe

I might be nearby, and that if I saw a reference to our old signal, I would come."

"It's very convenient, don't you think, that the sister of one of our primary researchers decided to make contact?"

Susan tried not to bristle at the quiet accusation in his tone. The career military officers who were attached to the project had a tendency to view everything in terms of whether or not it could be weaponized. There were other labs, she knew, dedicated more to practical applications than her own almost pure theoretical research, labs where they took things like the spectrum analysis of the impossible colors and tried to turn them into projections or EMP bursts that could be used to briefly take over local media channels and potentially incapacitate an enemy.

The first nation to figure out how to fully apply the lessons of the rifts to warfare was going to have an advantage that could not be overstated. Susan supposed she couldn't blame the military men for focusing on that side of the situation, even as she cursed them for complicating her science.

"No, sir," she replied stiffly. "I requested this position due to my history with the Evanston exclusion zone. My sister had good reason to believe I was attached to the research teams studying the area, and so she sent a signal she knew I'd understand. I don't believe she had any ulterior motive in making contact."

"Then why *did* she make contact, after seventeen years? All we've ever heard from the exclusion zones is that they would like to be left alone. What did she want?"

There was a dangerous glimmer in his eye, and Susan had to fight to remain still. The urge to squirm like a mouse cornered by a cat was strong, and she was smart enough to know he would devour her if she showed him any sign of weakness.

Susan looked him dead in the eye, and lied.

"She's dying," she said. "They believe lung cancer, given the progression of her symptoms and the difficulty she's having breathing. She wanted to see me again before she died, and was able to convince their governing council to allow her to make contact. I got the feeling it cost her quite a bit. I may or may not be able to make contact again."

"They have a form of government?"

"Yes." Lying was all well and good, but with the camera footage they had, they might be able to analyze the movement of Katharine's lips, even if there was no other recording to be picked apart and presented as proof that Susan was somehow working against the government of the United States. If she wanted to allay suspicion—even temporarily—she had to give them *something*. "They're self-organizing, because they've had to be. They're completely cut off, and most of them can't get out."

"We've seen people emerge from the Manhattan exclusion zone."

"Once, years ago. My sister said ongoing exposure to the leftover rift radiation has altered their biology such that they are no longer able to breathe outside the exclusion zones. I don't know whether this is true for all exclusion zones, or, if it is, whether the people inside would all have been modified in the same way." The urge to collect and dissect representative bodies from a variety of exclusion zones was strong, obscene, and entirely natural. She was a scientist. She wanted to *know*. "She can't cross the barrier. None of them can."

The gleam died. This was less useful than he'd been hoping, then; good. She wasn't in the mood to be particularly useful right now.

"So she just wanted to talk to her sister."

"Yes. I was able to ask many specific questions about what the incursion looked like from her side of the rift, and was in the process of documenting them when I was alerted to your arrival. If you don't mind, sir, I'd like to get back to work while as many of the details as possible are still fresh."

"Of course. Just one more thing, Dr. Black."

"Yes?"

"Why did you dispose of your phone and tablet?"

Susan stiffened, sensing the trap. "My sister was concerned about being recorded. Her children have been unwell. She wanted to review our family medical history, to discuss how likely it was that they have the same form of cancer she does. She was unwilling to do so in the presence of a recording device. Sir."

"I appreciate the desire to make your sister more comfortable, but you do understand that if this little encounter is to be repeated, we would like you to wear some sort of hidden recording device. The things you don't make note of may prove to be as important as the things you do."

"Yes, sir." Susan stood straighter, glad her hurry to get to the exclusion zone had been so obvious and so genuine. Any footage they pulled would show a woman in an obvious rush to get out of the building as quickly as possible. A somewhat delinquent youth and an adult employment by the United States government had taught her it was best to cloak her lies in as much of the truth as she could, and actions that created a veil of plausible deniability could sometimes be more powerful than the best excuses in the world.

"Will you be going back?" Susan didn't care for the hunger in his voice, but she kept her face carefully neutral.

"Only if she signals for me again, sir. I can't contact her, and she knows not to expect anything from my side of things." Telling him without coming out and saying it that setting up safety lights on their side of the barrier would do him no good at all.

From the look of disappointment that crossed his face, she could tell her message was duly received.

"I should go, sir," she said, trying to keep her voice gentle, like he wasn't her superior, like he couldn't command her to stay exactly where she was. "I want to finish writing down everything she said as soon as I can, to see if I can catch anything else in her story that I might have missed before. People sometimes say more than they meant to when they're talking to someone they haven't seen in a while." Not that her notes would mention anything about children, or cats, or dogs, or any of the other things she knew he would desperately want to know.

She couldn't hide everything. She couldn't conceal the fact that they'd met entirely. But she could make it as difficult for anyone to guess what she was planning as possible.

As if she were planning *anything* at this stage. She didn't know yet what she was going to do. She was just going to have to get there and see.

Susan looked calmly at the general and waited for him to say something. His next words would determine everything.

"Keep us informed, and if she signals you again, I want a whole team to go with you to the exclusion zone," he said.

"Yes, sir," she agreed, and turned and walked away, trying to look nonchalant, like she didn't want to break into a run and get to her work station as quickly as she possibly could, like all of this was perfectly normal.

Harris met her at the lab door. "The files you requested have come in," he said. "Why are you asking for histories on people living in impact zones?"

"Chasing a hunch."

How could she explain that she wanted to know whether there was a direct correlation between personal radiation levels and being able to cross the barrier safely? Clearly there was some unknown tipping point beyond which a person's tissues had become irradiated enough to permit passage, but did the radiation linger? Or did they eventually return to the human baseline? Would crossing the barrier and staying inside allow someone to acclimate sufficiently that they could remain in the exclusion zone, even if doing so caused their lungs to change and their biology to adapt?

Harris looked at her sharply. "A hunch sparked by your sister."

There was no point in lying to him. "Yes."

"That you're not going to tell me about, because you're trying to keep this as undocumented as possible."

Susan blinked, taken aback by his bluntness, but couldn't see a way around her answer. "...yes."

"I want in."

"What?"

"I said, I want in. You think I went into rift physics for fun?" He shrugged. "I want in."

"I interviewed you. There was nothing to indicate that you'd been impacted by the rifts."

"Well, then, your interview process wasn't thorough enough. My ex got married, and his wife had a baby in one of the impact zone hospitals. They named him after me. It made sense, since I was his godfather." Harris's mouth twisted. "Kid started setting fires with his brain when he was less than three years old, and the government made him disappear. He was a sweet kid. I want him back. So if you're going off the record, I want in."

Susan blinked again, more slowly this time, assessing him. This could be a trick: he could be working for the military, and trying to get her to incriminate herself. But it didn't make sense. The spies she'd had planted in her lab over the years—several at first, then fewer and fewer as it became clear that her work was unlikely to produce any assets that could be sold to foreign governments or turned into weapons for her own—had gone out of their way to be as subtle as possible, playing their cards close to their chests, keeping their heads down. They certainly didn't skulk around the lab like thieves for weeks without even making sure she knew their names.

She looked at him with new consideration. "Can you get me the family's medical records?"

"What?" He looked surprised, briefly. Then he nodded. "If that's what you need, I can email him. Dan and I are still on good terms."

"Then go ahead." Her smile was sharp and fleeting. "I need to get back to work."

Susan returned to her desk, and passed the rest of the afternoon in a haze of records and charts, comparing readings from around the country—and as much as possible, from around the world—looking for the commonalities she was after. It took some time to find them, as most equipment wasn't calibrated for the full range of possible radiation, and many of the reports had been dismissed as some kind of sensitivity failure. Eventually, however, she smacked her open palm against the desk.

"Harris!"

"Yes, Dr. Black?" His head popped up over the edge of his workspace, an attentive look on his sharp-featured face.

"I've found the commonality we need to scan for." His expression was politely blank, prompting her to continue. "Muons."

"Muons?"

"Yes."

"But those are—"

"Punishingly rare outside of particle accelerators, yes. Rare enough that we weren't even looking for them until we discovered the impact zones and started using more sensitive equipment in our scans." So much data lost to simple ignorance. But wasn't that the story of science throughout the ages? No point in crying over spilled milk. "The exclusion zones are surrounded by a muon shell. We've known that for quite some time. The impact zones also show an elevated muon level. It's not as compact, but it's present."

Susan's head was spinning. Had her sister just given her the key to the problem, accidentally and without intending it? If the increased muons were in some way connected to the reality distortions associated with the creatures, they could potentially begin measuring the strength of the impact zones. They could predict when they were going to dissolve. Assuming they ever would—muons were customarily measured in microseconds, exceptionally short-lived in comparison to anything other than another subatomic particle. For them to have lingered this long implied that something was generating them.

"How much time have you spent in impact zones?"

"You mean apart from working here?"

Susan nodded vigorously. Harris shrugged.

"I visited Dan and Mary while she was in the hospital, and went to see my godson right after he was born. Before that, I don't think I'd ever entered a documented impact zone. I've been here for about twelve hours a day, every day, for the last six months."

"Excellent. I don't have a hand-held muon detector..."

"Does *anyone* have a hand-held muon detector?"

"...but I think it might be possible to cobble one together from the equipment we already have."

"Is there a reason we need a hand-held muon detector?"

Susan smiled.

16.4.

"COBBLING TOGETHER" A way to detect a rare form of subatomic radiation outside the lab proved to be even more difficult than Susan had anticipated, and she found herself very glad for Harris, who had been an engineering minor and was a dab hand with a soldering gun. Even that wouldn't have been enough if one of the other grad students hadn't been working on a handheld cosmic ray detector for years. Harris lacked her grace with programming, but between the two of them and that unlucky student's life's work, they had a potentially functional device shortly after midnight. Susan looked at it and sighed.

"No time like the present," she said, before pointing it at him and taking a reading. "The normal human level of muon exposure is fewer than thirty particles per second. You're returning a level approximately ten thousand times that."

Harris raised his eyebrows. "Should I be alarmed?"

"It won't change anything if you are, so I wouldn't bother wasting the time if I were you." She handed him the reader, which was a square gunmetal box approximately the size of a traffic officer's radar gun. "Do me."

He pointed it, clicked, and waited, eyes widening as he got the reading. He didn't say anything, just clicked the trigger a second time, and then a third, before lowering the gun. "It's broken."

"If we're supposing that the impact zones are partially or wholly maintained by a new form of stable muon, it's not broken, no matter what it's saying. Although we do need to take into consideration the fact that we're inside an impact zone right now; that may be affecting our readings."

"It says your muon level is more than ten *million* times the human average!"

"We're looking at a very small particle, so it makes sense that any unusual accumulation would escalate very, very quickly." Susan tried to think of whether there had ever been any studies focusing on muon accumulation in the human body. She was fairly sure there hadn't been. There had been too many higher priorities since the incursion, and why would anyone have spent research funding on something that was genuinely impossible before the incursion when there were so many underfunded possibilities sitting around, waiting to be examined?

But possible had been canceled seventeen years ago, and they were living in the shadow of the impossible now.

"Grab your coat," she commanded, turning to snag her own bag and shove as many of her files into it as she could. The tendency to insist on paper printouts for certain materials had always seemed archaic and outdated to her. Now it seemed like a lifesaver. There was no point in taking her laptop, but she retrieved it anyway. The recording devices would catch her doing it, of course, but let them: they would know what she was up to soon enough, if they didn't know already.

Her masters had created a world where their own citizens couldn't trust them to help without trying to take over, where their primary goal after a world-changing natural disaster was not "how can we use this tragedy to make the world better" but "how can we use this to kill people more effectively?" She'd worked for the government for her entire adult life, as the only means of getting closer to her sister, and now that government was stealing children for the sole purpose of turning them into weapons, and she was done.

This was the night that Susan Black changed sides.

So she shoved her things into her bag and left the lab, Harris following behind her like a uniquely bipedal and obedient puppy, and no one stopped them. No one stopped them as they made their way down to the parking garage and to her private vehicle. She got behind the wheel and handed Harris the muon detector.

He blinked at her. "I need you to start taking readings once we're out of the impact zone," she said. "We're looking for concentrations not associated with any known impact or exclusion zones. Do you follow me?"

"You're thinking children like my godson will have a higher muon concentration," he said, slowly.

"Maybe. Maybe not. I don't have any superpowers, and I don't feel any coming on, assuming that getting ready to develop telekinesis is something you can *feel*. I didn't get a reading off of Kitty when we talked at the barrier, but she's been in the exclusion zone for seventeen years. Her muon level must be even higher than ours, and she doesn't have any abilities we don't. There's probably something else at play with the kids, something we can't pick up on yet. You're going to have to find a way to steer the research toward isolating a new set of subatomic particles if we want to understand that."

"What do you mean, I'm going to have to steer the research?"

Susan put the car into gear.

"Dr. Black, what do you mean I have to do it?"

"You're the one who'll be able to argue for the muon connection, and you'll have to say I coerced or forced you into going along with me tonight."

"I don't understand."

"Open the glove compartment if you would?"

Harris frowned before depressing the button. The glove compartment popped open.

"Hand me the little black case."

He did. She braced it between her knees and unzipped it before pulling out her handgun and aiming it squarely at his forehead. Harris paled.

"Dr. Black, you don't have to do this—"

"I do, though, because we're going to be passing a camera checkpoint in three, two, one." She smiled and lowered the gun. "I'm sorry about that, but I thought you might prefer not to join me when they put me on trial for treason."

"Treason? What are you talking about? What are you planning to do?"

"I can't find your godson for you, but I can help you find ways of finding him," said Susan. "I just need you to trust me for a little longer."

"Right now, I'm not feeling very trusting."

"I can understand that." They passed out of the impact zone, the invisible demarcation line separating what was apparently some unseen source of endless muons and the rest of the world. "All right. Start taking your readings now."

"It's not going to be easy from a moving car."

"That's true enough, but at this point we need to keep moving if we don't want them to stop us."

Harris looked at her anxiously before aiming the detector at the window. "All right. What am I looking for?"

"As I said before, I need you to scan for high muon concentrations not associated with any known incursion activity. We exhibit higher than normal muon levels, meaning..."

"Meaning they're transitive," he said, slowly. "Meaning exposure to the modified physical reality of the zones has caused us to somehow start generating a subatomic particle normally found in cosmic rays, and not in human tissues."

"Meaning people who've spent more time exposed will have higher levels than we do," said Susan grimly. She wanted those numbers. Oh, how she wanted those numbers. She was moving against her own government now; there was only so much time she could reasonably expect to have before they caught up with her. Knowing the muon concentration for safe passage into the exclusion zone might be the only thing that could possibly save her.

Whether or not she had consciously admitted it, Susan Black was already disengaging herself, piece by piece, from the life she'd created in Katharine's absence, and returning to the person she'd been built to be all along. The one who took chances; the one who didn't like rules. The one who only learned to follow them for the sake of finding her sister.

Susan wanted her back. Getting her was going to require more than wanting: it was going to need luck, and speed, and muons.

Muons were the answer.

Harris nodded, expression grim, and pulled the trigger, checking the readout. Susan continued to drive. The freeway they were on would gradually curve around the entire city, and then she'd start making her way through the interior, if they had that long. She was working under the assumption that one scientist going rogue and kidnapping a graduate student wouldn't necessitate an immediate public alarm; she might even be allowed to run for a while so that they could observe her and try to piece together what she'd learned that could make a good government employee turn like this.

What she'd learned was that the men who'd entered the Evanston exclusion zone to steal four children, including the niece and nephew she'd never met, had only shown up on one camera. Which wasn't just incredible opsec; it simply wasn't possible unless someone had been turning off the cameras for them, easing their way in.

What she'd learned was that even the partial license plate she'd been able to pull from the one camera where they *were* caught didn't show up in any databases; they were driving a ghost van, which took the likelihood of this entire situation not involving at least some kind of government collusion from "impossible" to "*fucking* impossible." This couldn't have happened without help.

There had never been any real chance the government wasn't involved. They'd been able to mostly quash stories about children born with superpowers—mostly, but not entirely; quashing anything entirely was impossible in this bright world of social media and constant documentation—but they couldn't conceal the fact that the birth rate near the spots where the monsters had died had gotten incredibly low, and the recorded rates of sudden infant death syndrome were incredibly high. If you lived in the shadow of a monsterfall, the rumors whispered, you'd probably never have a child, and if you did, they'd die before they took their first steps. The recorded births of superpowered children had been dropping off since those rumors started to spread.

Thinking about it, Susan realized she didn't remember the last time she'd seen a report verifying the transfer of custody from a family unit to the government. The United States at least still pretended to have ethics. Not every country did. Even the US didn't always. What was to stop someplace with less concern for the individual rights of citizens from setting up birthing camps in the impact zones, producing an endless stream of superhumans to exploit?

But the US, for all its failures of both civic responsibility and vision, still cared about optics, and they had yet to enforce any births inside the impact zones. Meaning they were losing a biological arms race they were still trying to understand. Meaning there would be implicit as well as explicit value in harvesting the children of the impact zones.

Susan had reason to know better than most how flexible the vaunted American ethics were when it came to that biological arms race, and they were more than flexible enough to allow for stealing children from people who didn't matter anymore, having long since been written off as casualties. People whose own families were unlikely to advocate for them, since none of those families knew they were still alive. The US government had stolen children from their parents before, when they thought they could get away with it, when the optics were somehow—even fleetingly—on their side.

Susan had some ideas about how the men who'd taken her sister's children had been able to move through the city unseen and survive entering the exclusion zone. The only real question she had was whether they had somehow acquired sufficient muon levels on their own, or whether there was a piece of technology that she was missing—a piece of technology she now desperately desired.

Harris whistled. She glanced at him. "What?"

"Muon concentration to the northwest. It's showing as a full order of magnitude higher than yours. The display can't handle the number. I'm getting an *error* where the readout should be." He sounded personally offended by that error.

"Then that's where we're going." She was going to end this. One way or another, she was going to bring those children home.

CHAPTER 25: **KIDNAPPERS**

25.1.

Harris kept taking readings as Susan drove, helping her close in, bit by bit, on a narrow downtown street. They were in the heart of urban Chicago now, surrounded by steel and masonry, and human lives. Susan hadn't been this close to this many people in years, and her skin crawled as she pulled onto the final block.

"There," said Harris with some certainty, pointing at a building whose lower floor appeared to have been converted into a dental practice. The lights were on, and what Susan could see through their window was white and clean and brightly lit. Sterile.

Probably terrifying to children who'd grown up inside an exclusion zone, who'd been snatched from their parents and carried to a place that couldn't have seemed more alien.

Susan kept driving, scanning for a parking place.

"What are we doing here?" asked Harris finally.

She'd brought him into this. She had to trust him. Turning to face him, Susan said, "My sister made contact because her children were stolen by men from our side of the barrier who had been able to cross into the exclusion zone without being killed by the zone's defenses. They seemed to know the layout inside the zone better than can be explained with any surveillance technology we have access to, and they only showed up on one of the local camera feeds. She wants her kids back. I believe the muons provide protection on the other side of the barrier, and the higher your concentration, the easier it is to both cross and survive. So the men who took the kids would have to possess extremely high muon concentrations."

Harris was a quick study, she'd give him that. He blinked once before his face hardened and he said, "You think the government figured out the muons a while ago and has hidden the information."

"All it would have taken is a few more finely calibrated detectors and someone with a background in particle physics to make them aware of it."

"So they can pass in and out of the exclusion zones at will."

"Maybe not at will. It depends on whether they've created some kind of generator to accelerate muon concentration in the people involved." She pulled up to the curb at the end of the block, turning off the engine. "But they're stealing children. The people in that building are stealing children, children who won't have parents or families to advocate for them, children the world doesn't know exist. They'll sell them as weapons to the United States government, and this is our only chance to save them. I understand if you don't want to come with me. Leave the muon detector, tell the military I held you at gunpoint and you ran as soon as you got the chance. You can build another detector. You can go looking for your godson. Or you can stay and help me save my niece and nephew."

Harris nodded, slowly. "I know we don't know each other very well, Dr. Black, but that is the most offensive thing you've ever said to me."

Susan raised her eyebrows and said nothing.

"The idea that I'd run when there are children in danger is…I don't have words for how ugly that is. Of course I'm going to help you. If our government is doing this, I need to know, and I need to find another way to complete my studies. Because no degree is worth helping people hurt kids. I'm in this until it's over."

Susan smiled.

25.2.

THERE WAS NO need to creep along the street. Attempting to skulk would have just drawn more attention, and as Susan still wasn't completely sure what she was going to do when they found the kids—or worse, the culprits—she didn't want to attract attention before she had to. So they walked, side by side, heads tilted toward each other, trying to look like a young couple out for a stroll in a largely business-zoned part of town. Maybe they were heading for one of the local restaurants, or to walk around a small park whispering sweet nothings in each other's ears.

Or maybe they were having a dental emergency, since they swerved toward the dentist's office as soon as they reached it, trying the door and looking disappointed when they found it locked. The man of the pair looked up and down the street, maybe checking for help, maybe looking for witnesses, as the woman got on her knees and tugged him toward her. On the cameras, it looked as if they'd actually been seeking a spot for a private assignation, and had simply decided to perform their private acts in the middle of a city street.

Stepping into place to shield Susan as much from view as possible, Harris asked, "What are you doing?"

"I don't think we've ever discussed our respective rebellious youths," said Susan, pulling a pin out of her hair, tamed as it always was into a perfectly respectable, businesslike bun. "I was the wild child of my family. Constantly in trouble. It was my sister's job to pull me back, and well, an exclusion zone ate her when it killed our parents, so I'm sure you can guess how much trouble I got into between the incursion and graduate school."

"You stopped getting into trouble when you hit graduate school?" asked Harris numbly. He was starting to feel like he'd fallen into some sort of action movie, and he wasn't sure how he was supposed to feel about that. Or whether he was going to survive.

"No." The smile she slanted up at him was practically feral, and only the fact that recoiling would show her to the world kept him from stepping away. He'd never seen that look on her face before. He wasn't sure he wanted to be seeing it now. "I stopped getting *caught* when I hit graduate school. I was going to do whatever it took to get into the Evanston exclusion zone and find my sister. That meant getting a job in one of the government labs and proving I could be a respectable researcher. It meant leading my own team and proving our work was essential. I could have played along better—could have focused more on things that could be used to kill people—but I did what I could without making the world worse. And none of that changed who I actually was."

The whole time she was talking, she was working the end of her pin into the lock, twisting it gently back and forth.

"The thing most people get wrong about this is the force required. If the lock is simple enough that you can pop it with a pin, you don't want to try too hard. You'll just break your bobby pin off inside the mechanism, and then *nobody* can use the door anymore. It's bad pool." As she spoke, there was a soft click, and the door swung gently inward. She smiled up at Harris, then bent the pin sharply, breaking the last inch or so of it off inside the mechanism, as she had predicted. "Oops. Guess nobody can use this lock. Let's go."

Harris stepped back as she rose. "You're even scarier than I thought you were, and I've been terrified of you since my first day in your lab."

"Who, me? I'm just a sweet little government scientist who accidentally broke her bobby pin." She pushed the door further open, pulling the handgun out of her pocket. "Shall we go greet our hosts?"

"Are they hosts when we're not invited?"

"I don't know. Do people usually invite tapeworms?" She stepped through the open door, smiling at Harris the whole time, and after a moment's stunned staring, he followed.

The lobby was empty. That much had been obvious from the outside. There was a desk cordoning off a small reception area, with seats and work stations for up to three people, and a door on the wall opposite, presumably leading deeper into the practice. The specific nature of the office played against the kidnappers, at this stage: like most dental offices, this one had clearly been sound sculpted by a professional, with acoustics designed to keep the patients who were still waiting for their appointments from hearing the drills and sounds of distress from deeper in.

Harris held up the muon detector and aimed it at the door before pulling the trigger. The same reading as before came back. There was definitely at least one person with an abnormal muon count deeper in the practice. They were not alone.

He showed the screen to Susan, who nodded before creeping quietly forward and testing the knob. This one turned easily, and when she pushed the door, it swung inward without a sound.

Susan and Harris slipped deeper inside, out of view from the street, heading toward an unseen enemy.

They were only halfway down the hall when the sound of sniffling broke the quiet, followed by a man's voice growling, "Will somebody shut that brat up?"

"How long do we have to hold them here?" asked a second man.

"Until Anderson sends his people to pick them up," said the first. "He's got us on a pretty close timeline, but apparently one of his researchers has a sister inside the exclusion zone, and she could become a problem. He needs to be sure she's out of play before he approves the pickup."

"That's *General* Anderson to you," said a third voice.

The first snorted. "Not anymore it's not."

Harris looked at Susan, who was practically vibrating with anger, looking oddly relieved at the same time. The three men had just confirmed that they were either military or ex-military, and working for the same man who was in charge of Susan's lab. Meaning, among other things, that General Anderson had had access to whatever means of surveillance they were using inside the exclusion zone.

Meaning he had known her sister was alive, and had withheld that information, presumably to guarantee Susan wouldn't interfere with whatever he was planning for the exclusion zone and its inhabitants. It was a betrayal of everything they'd been told their research stood for, and he could see the fury brewing in her eyes. He put a hand on her arm, shaking his head as he tried to signal her to stay where she was. There were at least three of them, if not all four, and two were current or former military. She had a gun. He didn't. This wouldn't go well for them.

And none of that mattered to her right now. She shrugged his hand off and strode briskly forward, shoving open the final door between them and the voices, gun raised and firmly pointed toward the people on the other side.

"Hi," she said, in a tone that was bright and chipper and laced with menace. "I work for General Anderson, too. And I don't believe those children belong to you."

25.3.

THE EXAM ROOM was small enough to be a tight fit for three adult men and four children, made slightly less claustrophobic—at least for the men—by the fact that all four children were tied up, hands held in front of them with loops of electrical tape, more tape plastered over their mouths. They ranged in age from around six to a young twelve, all clean, dressed in clothes that looked to Harris like they'd barely been rescued from the garbage heap. "Threadbare" wasn't even close to good enough to describe their condition.

The oldest of them appeared to be unconscious, slumped against his bonds and not moving at all.

The men, on the other hand, were wearing black combat gear, and sporting the close-cropped hairstyles he'd long since come to associate with career military. They were looking at the woman in the doorway with vaguely academic interest, like she was some kind of fascinating insect that had flown into the room to distract them, and not an armed scientist who was actually pointing a gun at them.

"I recognize you," said one of the men, in a quizzical tone. "You work at that lab they set up in the old hospital, down where the monster fell. You're that crazy science lady whose sister is in the zone, right? What, you're here because one of these brats is hers?" He bellowed laughter, like he'd just said the funniest thing in the world.

He was still laughing when Susan pulled the trigger. He fell without another sound, taken so completely by surprise that he had no time to react. The other two men were not so distracted, and one of them drew his gun. Not fast enough to avoid taking a bullet to the throat and joining his friend.

The third man rose from his seat and lunged for the counter where his gun and some of their equipment had been stacked. Harris grabbed a tray of dental instruments that had been left out nearby—and he couldn't imagine that was particularly hygienic—and slung it at the man as hard as he could.

It hit him in the chest, not stopping him, but distracting him from his goal as he glanced involuntarily toward Harris. That was all the time Susan needed. She fired again, and the third kidnapper fell. The room went silent, save for the sounds of children breathing and whimpering around their masks. Susan stayed where she was, gun still raised, eyes flicking to the corners like the fourth man might appear at any moment.

"Susan," said Harris urgently. She didn't respond. "*Susan*," he repeated, more sharply. She turned, slowly, to look at him.

He didn't like that, since her turn brought the gun along as a horrible bonus, but it was better than her tense, anxious stillness.

"You can put the gun down now," he said. "You killed them."

Three men who had been alive moments before, who had been paid by someone—presumably their own boss—to kidnap four children from inside the exclusion zone, were dead now. Maybe they hadn't deserved to die for it, but his own government had openly committed the same crime when they snatched Harris Jr. out of his mother's arms because of where he'd been born. Harris didn't even know if the boy was still alive, had had no way of knowing in four years. If he could have killed the men who'd taken him, he would have done it with his bare hands to punish them for the crime of taking that boy, of putting that look in Mary's eyes.

He supposed Susan had seen that same expression in her sister's eyes when they spoke across the barrier. And thinking of it like that, he could understand why she'd been able to murder the first man in cold blood.

Susan finally seemed to see her surroundings and lowered the gun, clicking the safety back on before she returned it to her pocket. "The children," she gasped, and rushed to kneel beside them. "I'm so sorry you had to see that," she said. "It wasn't right, and I'm sorry."

One of them, a little girl who looked about nine years old, stared solemnly at Susan as she produced a pocket knife from the depths of her pocket and flipped it open, using it to saw through the tape holding the child's wrists and ankles together. This achieved, Susan moved on to the next, allowing the girl to peel the tape off of her own mouth.

"Are you my auntie?" the girl asked, once the tape was off.

Susan stiffened, almost slicing her own finger in surprise. "Are you Kitty's daughter? Are you Susan?" she asked.

"I am."

"Then yes. I'm your aunt. You were named after me." Tears stung her eyes, making it difficult to see as she moved to the third child, cutting him free. "Which one of you is Vincent?"

"The bad men stuck him with a pin and he went asleep," said Susan. "He's been asleep since they did that."

"They must have injected him with some sort of sedative," said Harris. "Probably not dental. Those are designed to wear off quickly, since people come for appointments during the work day, but there are other things on the market."

All three of the children turned to look at him, wary and tense, like wild things backed into the corner of their den by a larger predator.

"He's with me," said Susan. "This is Harris, who works in my lab. Do you know what a lab is?"

The two children who weren't related to her shook their heads. The younger Susan nodded. "Mom always says she wanted to work in one before the world changed. You have a lab?"

"I do," said Susan. "Do they call you 'Susan'? Or do they call you something shorter?"

"Vincent calls me 'Susie,' and I guess it's okay," said Susie. "Is *he* going to be okay?" Flickers of color were beginning to flash and spiral in her pupils, impossible colors, colors that weren't meant to be seen by human eyes, much less contained by them.

"I don't want to lie to you," said Susan. "I don't know. I didn't even know if you'd be able to breathe outside the boundary. But I'm going to do my best to make sure he—"

Something slammed from behind them. Something that sounded like a door banging open. Susan stiffened, reaching for her gun. "Harris?"

"On it." He eased the door to their room closed, but not before they heard booted footsteps moving down the hall. "They must have followed you."

"Of course they followed me," hissed Susan. She positioned herself in front of the children, gun in hand. "I have three more bullets. Does the door lock?"

"Yes," verified Harris.

"So lock it! Buy us a few more seconds before they get here."

"It's all right, Aunt Susan," said Susie dreamily. The colors in her eyes were spiraling faster and faster, spreading out of her pupils and into her irises, swallowing them whole.

The door slammed open.

Harris yelled as men in military blacks poured into the room, guns in their hands and boots heavy on the floor.

A gun went off.

It wasn't Susan's.

Susan fell.

Susie stood, the colors in her eyes finally swallowing them completely, erasing the distinction between iris, pupil, and sclera.

The men kept coming.

Susie smiled at them. "No," she said, voice calm and very clear.
And
Everything
Changed.

CHAPTER 36: SECOND INCURSION

36.1.

Harris had managed to fall back when the men came crashing into the room, and was thus, if only barely, on the side of the room with Susan and the children when Susie walked toward the intruders, the air in front of her rippling like heavy honey, filled with the promise of crashing storms. The men yelled, and some of them fired their guns, but the bullets dissolved into the heavy air, breaking down into their component molecules and drifting away as harmless vapors.

"Naughty," said Susie. "Naughty, naughty."

Susan was on the floor, Susan was bleeding. Harris dropped to his knees and crawled toward her, pulling her into his arms and frantically searching for the wound.

"Shoulder," she hissed. "Through and through. If you can stop the bleeding, I'll be fine."

The men were still yelling, their voices reduced to distorted static by the rippling air splitting the room in two. Sound didn't seem to carry well through the barrier, such as it was. Susan looked at it, face going slack with wonderment where before it had been tight with pain.

"I've seen this before," she said. "Oh, those fools. Those stupid, short-sighted *fools*."

"What?"

She tilted her head back to look at him. "We've asked a lot about where the incursions came from, why they happened, what purpose they served. We never considered that they might not have even known we were here. They were running away."

"From what?"

"Themselves."

And the air ripped open, suddenly filled with the same glorious, impossible colors as Susie's eyes, and the black dome of a barrier came into being between the men and the cowering pile of children and scientists, and the second incursion was begun.

36.2.

SUSIE DIDN'T LIKE it here.

The air smelled funny outside the barrier. It smelled like the old things they sometimes found when they explored a new building, scavenging deeper and deeper into areas that had once been deemed unstable and off limits. It smelled like chemicals she didn't have names for, and everywhere she looked there were too many people moving too quickly, all of them bright and flashy in ways that were guaranteed to attract predators. She didn't understand how anyone could live very long, Outside. It seemed like a death world.

She'd even seen some people walking with dogs on leashes. Dogs! Like it could ever be a good idea to yoke yourself to something that dangerous and unpredictable. Sometimes Mom talked about dogs being friends, and they were different in the old books she'd read, but she'd seen people swallowed up by dogs before, and it wasn't a pretty way to die. At least cats were mostly harmless if you were bigger than them. No one but babies had to be afraid of cats, unless there were kittens nearby. Cats didn't think so clear when they thought their kittens might be in danger.

No, she didn't like it Outside one bit, and nothing she'd seen since they got here made her like it any more. The men who'd taken them had put a needle in Vincent's arm and he'd gone asleep, and he still wouldn't wake up. They'd done it because the first three times they tried to bind his hands he'd just moved through the tape they'd wrapped around him. That was Vincent's special: he could go through things like they weren't there. He said he could see how much space there was inside every solid thing, and just convinced that space it should let him through. He didn't like to do it too much, though, because every time he did he remembered how much space there was inside of him, and it made him feel a little sick, like one day he might try to come back together and not be able to figure out the way to.

But these men had come to steal them from their mom and their home and they'd been determined to take all four of them—Vincent and Marcos and Angie because they had good and useful specials that maybe people could use to do things, and Susie because she was Vincent's sister, and even though no one had ever seen her special, everyone assumed she had to have a pretty good one.

She did. She had the *best* special, and no one knew it but her and Vincent and her mom.

Her dad used to know it, too. She'd never forgotten the night he found out. He'd yelled so loud their mom had yelled back, and Mom *never* yelled, and then he'd grabbed his jacket and left, and Mom had followed him out into the night.

Mom had come back. Dad never had. Susie had never seen him again, anywhere, and there had been dogs howling that night and all the way until morning, dogs, and the horrible wet sounds they made when they ate. Mom had never told them what had happened out there that night, where Dad had gone, but Susie had her suspicions.

She knew Mom would always keep her safe. But no one could know about her special.

And so those men hadn't known, when they took her, and they hadn't known when they hurt her brother, and they hadn't known when they called her bad words, and they hadn't known when her aunt had broken into the room like some sort of avenging hero and shot them all down dead, one by one. And these men didn't know, either, because no one knew, no one was allowed to know unless it was show them or die. Her mom had been very firm on that. She could show her special if she was afraid she might not be alive anymore if she kept it secret.

All these men had guns. They had already shot Aunt Susan, blood on the floor and in the air, and so she had good reason to be afraid she might not be alive anymore if she didn't show them. And it was hard to have a secret so big and so important and not tell anyone, so part of her was even sort of happy, because she was finally showing someone her special.

She had the *best* special.

Vincent could look at things and see how much space there was between them, but Susie could look at nothing and see how many of the special dots were there, both kinds, the ones everybody had and the ones that were just for kids like her. She liked the ones that were just for kids best of all. They were colors nobody had names for (nobody but her, because she gave them names, and whispered them to herself at night before she fell asleep, a catechism of one, first psalm of the church of the incursion) but that all the kids with specials had stuck all over them. Mom had a few, too. Most of the adults did. Not too many, though; not enough to give them a special of their own.

Susie couldn't move the special dots, not the way Marcos could—and no one knew that yet but her, not even Marcos, because he couldn't see the special dots the way she could, and she wasn't allowed to tell anyone what she saw, what she could do—but she could call for more of them, and pull the air open to see what was on the other side.

Dad had caught her doing it on the night he went away, and he'd been madder than she'd ever seen him be before. He'd screamed at her that what she was doing was how this whole nightmare started in the first place, and then he'd hit her, his hand across her face, stinging slap with a sound like thunder, and she hadn't been able to breathe, she hadn't been able to breathe, she'd been so scared that she'd lost her hold on the air around the special dots, and the little hole she'd tugged open had slammed shut, and then Mom had been there, and they'd been yelling.

And she was pretty sure Mom had killed Dad and let the dogs have what was left of him. Mom didn't have a special, but she had a gun, even though no one but the council was supposed to have guns and Mom hadn't been on the council for two whole summers, and when the gun spoke, people had to listen. Dad had never liked to listen.

Susie was pretty sure he'd listened one last time, because Mom hadn't given him a choice.

Vincent had been sad for a long time after Dad left. Susie hadn't been. Every time she tried to be sad, she just remembered his hand across her face, how much it had hurt her, how tears had sprung to her eyes because it hurt so bad. Maybe it wasn't right for someone to die because they'd hit somebody else just once, but she thought it might be different when it was a parent and a child. Maybe when a parent hit a child, they deserved whatever happened next.

Parents were supposed to protect you, the way Mom protected her. They were supposed to keep you safe, and never, never hurt you, or they weren't really parents. So Dad wasn't really her father, and if the dogs wanted him, they could have him.

There weren't as many special dots on this side of the barrier as there were on the other side, but there were enough for her to grab hold of, using them as posts to hammer into the air while she pulled it apart on either side, until the special dots were glowing beacons in an infinite space, until there was nothing but blackness and the swirling colors between her and the men, until she couldn't even see the men anymore.

She heard their guns go off, loud as anything, but there were no bullets. The special dots stopped them from getting any farther than the barrier, pulling them apart. Only special things could pass through one of her openings. She could go through, she knew that instinctively, and Vincent, but not Mom, and that was why she'd never go. She wasn't going to leave her mother like that. They needed each other too much.

But she pulled and pulled, until it felt like there wasn't any special left in her, until it felt like everything she was or would ever be was stretched into the air, holding that hole open. She couldn't feel the size of the tear she'd made, but she knew it was big. The biggest ever. She hadn't even known she could make a hole this big.

The man who'd come into the room with Aunt Susan stood slowly, Aunt Susan's blood on his hands, and stared at the colors swirling in the air. "Holy shit," he breathed.

"You said a swear," said Angie primly. She had moved so that she was right next to Aunt Susan. She took the older woman's hand in hers, and asked, "Can I take it away?"

Susan looked into the little girl's eyes, which were a deep, beautiful brown with tiny flecks of impossible aurora caught at the edges of the iris, and she nodded. "You can," she said. She didn't know what she was agreeing to, but she hoped. Given some of the things she'd seen the children of the impact zones accomplish, given what Susie was doing in front of them right now, oh, she hoped.

"Thank you," said Angie, and let go of Susan's hand, moving her own hands to the wound in Susan's shoulder and pushing down against it, until the pain was a sheet of incandescent fire, blazing through every cell in Susan's body, until there was nothing left *but* pain. Her eyes squinted shut involuntarily, no longer able to stay open in the face of dizzying, sickening agony.

Angie took her hands away. The pain went with her. Susan gasped and sat up, moving her shoulder to test it. There was no pain. No bullet hole, either. She was perfectly unwounded, and she stared at the child, who shrugged, looking faintly abashed.

"It's my special," she said. "Mama says one day nobody'll ever need to worry about dying from anything but getting old or being stupid, because of me and kids like me. I don't know from that. I just know I don't like when people are hurting. It itches."

Susan nodded slowly, forcing herself not to look away, not to stare at her niece, who was standing in front of the cascading wall of colors and hazy blackness with her hands slightly raised and her head cocked to the side, like she was watching a movie. She couldn't risk breaking the girl's concentration, and she didn't want to look at the swirling veil long enough to risk her own mind.

"Does anyone else hurt right now?" she asked. "Anyone close enough for you to feel."

She was mostly concerned about the still-unconscious Vincent, who had been dosed with something unidentified by men who didn't see him as a human child, but as a potential asset. Would they have been careful with him? Had they done permanent damage?

"One of the bad mens you shot hurts a lot, but he'll be dead soon, and we won't have to worry about him," said the girl.

Susan stiffened. "Okay, honey, that's good to know. What's your name?"

"I'm Angie."

"Okay, Angie. If he starts to move or feel like he's going to do something that's not dying, I want you to yell for me right away, and I'll make sure he stops." Susan pushed herself off the floor. "Harris, I want you to look at me now."

"Do you *see* what she's doing?" he asked, not taking his eyes away from the barrier, covered as it was with beautiful, swirling colors. "Do you *see* it?"

"Harris, I am your superior, and you *will* look at me now."

Reluctantly, he dragged his eyes away from the spectacle and focused on her, frowning. "What? Why do I need to be looking at you to have a conversation? You've never been this hung up on eye contact."

"Kitty never liked it, so I got out of the habit of forcing it on people," said Susan. "You, however, need to be looking at me now because if you look at the pretty swirly impossible colors for too long, you will die. Either as soon as the colors go away, or when your eyes melt out of your skull."

Harris blinked. "What?"

"Kitty told me about it. It's what happened to people on her side of the barrier when the first rifts closed."

"Is this…"

"I think so, yes." Susan nodded. "It looks like my niece has opened a rift, just like the ones that started this whole thing. And we just have to hope the things that came out of the first rifts were able to do so because they had opened them, and not because the rifts open onto a dimension of infinite monsters."

Harris paled. "You can't mean that."

"Can't I?" Susan waved toward the black, chromatic wall. How it managed to be both at the same time was enough to give her a headache, but she didn't want to look any closer to try puzzling out the mechanism. She believed her sister. Kitty had no reason to lie to her. "We can't see what's happening on the other side, but those men aren't screaming anymore. Doesn't that seem like a bad thing to you? Because it seems like a bad thing to me."

Harris frowned and closed his eyes, turning toward the barrier. She could see by the tension in his neck and jaw that he was listening as hard as he could. She did the same.

No screams came through.

36.3.

ON THE OTHER side of the barrier, the men who'd been sent to retrieve two of Anderson's wayward eggheads—and leave it to the man to lose track of his researchers during the first major extraction from the local exclusion zone; he'd be stripped of his rank soon enough if he didn't get himself under control—shrank back in horror from the wavering tear that had opened in the fabric of reality. Then, when it did nothing but hang there, spreading at a slow but geometric rate, the air around it alight with tiny blue-white flashes, like someone was striking a flint against a stone they couldn't see, they began to relax.

No monsters were coming through. Nothing was happening beyond the blackness, and the blackness was simple enough. The colors were fascinating, indescribably beautiful, impossible to name or understand.

They weren't here for beauty. Michael Wilson, who had been sent to lead this little retrieval mission, pointed to two of his men and then at the center of the rift. They shot him near-identical looks of terrified confusion, shaking their heads. He nodded exaggeratedly and pointed again.

It's said that self-preservation is one of the most basic of impulses, and like any basic impulse, it can be squashed and redirected by sufficient training. These men wanted to survive. They had been taught, in some cases for years, that what they wanted was less important than what their government wanted from them. If Sergeant Wilson was telling them to go into the blackened, swirling veil, they would go.

Rising up, they adjusted their grips on their guns and charged for the tear, half-expecting, in the absence of the monsters, to run through in under a step and emerge on the other side, where a woman with a handgun, an unarmed student, and four children waited.

Five men plunged into the tear, leaving only their sergeant behind.

None of them emerged again.

For them, their first step carried them into burning cold, striking and searing their lungs, freezing the small hairs of their nostrils almost instantly. The second step carried them through the barrier, as they had hoped it would, and onto a blasted landscape of shifting stones split through with veins of molten rock. The sky was alight with twists of black and burning clouds, spinning and spiraling against a background of red and orange, like somewhere a fire was burning so brightly that it lit up the entire world.

They gaped, falling into a circular formation without a second thought, backs to one another to cut off as many avenues of attack as possible, faces tilted uniformly toward that terrible sky. Private Jordan Lewis found himself closest to the point where they had emerged. There was no veil here, no tear, no twisting vortex of impossible colors. Instead, there was a faint shimmer, like the surface of a soap bubble. He reached out, and his hand passed through that impossible coldness again before emerging out the other side.

(Sergeant Wilson, who had just watched all five of his men charge into nothingness and vanish without a sound, stared as the hand protruded back through the tear in the surface of the world, fingers spread in a beseeching gesture. The skin was already beginning to melt away, dripping down like wax. He didn't take the offered hand. He didn't follow its owner through the tear. He simply stared, unable to quite move.)

Private Lewis pulled his hand back, and began screaming as he saw the wreckage of his skin, the way it was dripping down to reveal flesh and gleaming white connective tissue. There was no blood. It was as if his epidermis had been stripped cleanly and painlessly away.

He barely had time for that thought to form before the pain began. He howled in open agony as the wind lashed against the exposed nerve endings of his hand, abrading it with countless tiny particles of nothingness.

The rest of his skin was still intact, and none of the rest of them seemed to be melting. Passage into this unspeakable hellscape was safe, but going back was death.

Lewis clutched at his wrist with his unmelted hand, screams becoming howls of agony as the exposed tissue began to liquify and drip after his skin, leaving bare, exposed bone.

"Shut him up," said one of the other men, with some urgency.

Lewis continued howling.

"Shut him *up*," repeated the man, and pointed to the sky, where a vast flying reptile that could have easily been called a dragon if dragons had been a real thing that actually existed and weren't just creatures out of fantasy stories, was flying in vast and lazy loop-de-loops. It was too big to fly. Its wings couldn't possibly have been sufficient to hold its massive body aloft. The man, whose name was Benjamin Alvarez, vaguely remembered a lecture wherein he had been told, along with a room of bored men who just wanted to get out of the classroom and back to basic training, that the creatures from the other side of the rifts had somehow managed to carry bubbles of their own physical space with them. They had literally rewritten the laws of the universe to allow their own survival.

He'd thought that was just something they said to excuse the universal failure of the world's military forces when faced with unexpected, unexplainable monsters. Now, staring at this thing that shouldn't—couldn't—exist, he realized that they hadn't been stating the situation clearly enough. These creatures traveled with their own physics because there was no other possible way they could have crossed into Earth's reality and lived.

Lewis's howls were dwindling into low, petrified moans. Alvarez glanced at the man. Even the bones of his hand were gone now, replaced by a jutting stump that was beginning to ooze slow, dark blood. The blood should have been spurting, jetting out at a high speed. The fact that it wasn't meant that something was probably wrong with the wound, but there wasn't time to worry about that now, not with the…call it a dragon, nothing else came even close to describing the thing. Not with the dragon circling above them, its attention apparently having been caught by the screaming before it dwindled.

It swooped down, and the beating of its wings was the coming of a terrible storm. The scent of rotting meat and brimstone radiated off its terrible body as it swept down low, clawed feet open to snatch and tear. It roared, high and shrill and terrible.

When it snatched at them, it missed, and momentum carried it forward through the rift, disappearing. Alvarez straightened, having crouched instinctively when the thing flew by overhead, and turned to stare silently at the empty space in front of the soap bubble sheen of the rift.

"They can go through, but we can't go home," breathed another of the men. "We can't go *home.*"

Alvarez turned on him, frowning. "Calm yourself, soldier. We may be able to find another way. They came through once, there has to be a way for us to do the same. Remain strong and stalwart, and we'll find a way home."

Lewis, his right arm now missing all the way to the elbow, whimpered, but said nothing. Out of all of them, he had experienced the consequences of trying to go home. He wasn't going to push his luck trying again. More of his body was crumbling away with every second that passed, and the pain was both intense and indescribable. He wasn't sure the agonies were ever going to stop, and if they didn't...if they didn't, it might be worth charging through the rift again. Better to melt away entirely than to dissolve inch by terrible inch.

He also wasn't sure how much longer his head would remain clear enough to make that a choice. The pain was starting to nibble at the edges of his sanity, even as the creeping dissolution was nibbling at the edges of his flesh. Soon enough, he'd break, and then he'd run in whatever direction seemed likely to make the hurting stop. Chasing the pretty rainbows in the air was as good of an idea as anything else.

Alvarez was still speaking, something brave and stirring and inspirational, no doubt, something to make this situation seem survivable. Lewis stared at him with wide, agonized eyes, trying to hear the sense behind the sounds. It refused to come.

What *did* come was a section of the ground behind him, shifting upward with such exquisite, impossible slowness that at first Lewis thought he was starting to hallucinate, rising onto what were increasingly visible as short, narrow legs. They weren't stubby, for all that the creature, even once it was fully upright, was not tall: they were surprisingly delicate, and there were a lot of them. It didn't look like a giant millipede, despite the number of legs involved: it was more like a vast, multi-limbed salamander.

Some of the other men had noticed it. They nudged each other and muttered, staring. Alvarez broke off in the middle of his grand speech and scowled at them.

"Well?" he demanded. "What is it?"

One of the men pointed. He began to turn.

He didn't finish the gesture, or at least, not all of him did. He was gone from the waist up before he could fully turn, and the salamander creature was looking at the rest of them with speculation in its flat black eyes. It swallowed, and the top half of Alvarez was gone, taking whatever he'd been about to say with it.

Apparently, Alvarez met with approval, because the salamander-thing swallowed and surged forward, gulping down another of the men before he had a chance to scream, leaving Lewis and two more—he thought Mallory and Christianson, but he wasn't sure, the pain was blurring their faces. It was also preventing panic from surging in, and he thought he might be a little bit grateful for that, especially as the story was now clearly written in the seconds yet to come. He could see it like a script floating in the air.

Well. There was one thing he could still do. The people who'd sent them here—Wilson, who'd stayed safely behind when they plunged into the blackness of the rift—they'd known, on some level, what they were doing. They'd been aware. They messed with forces they should never have messed with, and they'd brought this down on themselves.

They deserved to pay for what they'd done. That was the main thought echoing through Private Lewis's already-dissolving mind as he spun around and charged toward the rainbow shining in the air.

Back in the dentist's office, Sergeant Wilson was still staring in rapt shock at the swirling rainbow wall of the rift when Private Lewis came charging back through the veil. One of his sleeves dangled empty, a flapping tube of fabric, and his face began to drip down in waxen rivulets almost before he was completely through. Still, he kept running, even though he must have been in unbelievable agony. Wilson was almost impressed, in the few seconds he had before the giant salamander emerged from the rift behind the fleeing man, mouth open, ready to devour.

The literal fucking dragon that had plunged through only a moment before had destroyed much of the roof, creating an opening onto a sky split with lightning bolts and riddled through with clouds. The salamander—easily the size of a bus, if not actually larger—took out the wall. Wilson was spared the indignity of being devoured when he was crushed to death, collapsing to the floor and dying almost instantly.

The salamander snapped its jaws closed around the dissolving body of Private Lewis and continued forward, away from the rift, into the unprepared and undefended night. Everything was silent inside the office, save for the crackle of broken lights, the spark of torn electrical wires. In the far distance, something exploded. Sirens wailed. If there were screams—and logic said that there were almost certainly screams—they were too distant to hear.

Behind the barrier, Susie was starting to droop. Susan looked at her, anxious, then to Angie. "Angie, does Susie hurt?" she asked.

"No," said Angie.

The boy who hadn't been sedated piped up for the first time. "She's almost out of special."

"What does that mean?"

He bit his lip and shied away, clearly frightened of Susan's voice. She swore inwardly, but didn't say anything else. He'd been kidnapped from his home by armed men, and the first he'd seen of her, she'd been shooting those same men. He'd seen nothing of adults outside the barrier that would make him feel like he could trust them, and quite a bit to confirm that no, he couldn't.

Susan moved away from Harris, still not looking at the colors dancing through the barrier, and stepped up behind Susie. "Susie, can you talk to me, sweetie?"

"I can," said Susie, voice dreamy and distant. "It hurts, Aunt Susan."

"What hurts?"

"Holding it open. I've never done one so big before, and it feels like it's vibrating, and it hurts."

"Can you let it close?"

"I can't, I can't!" said the girl, voice peaking into a wail. "If the bad men are still there, they'll hurt us, and I don't want anyone to get hurt."

"No, honey, no. You're a child. I'm the adult. You don't have to protect us. Let me protect you. I have my gun. If the bad men are still there, they're going to be very busy trying to figure out what to do with what you've made. They won't expect us. You can let it close." Inwardly, Susan was afraid there might be another meaning to "I can't," that Susie might not be able to seal the rift again. But the girl was shaking harder with every passing moment, and if she was going to maintain the control to close it, it had to happen now.

"You're safe with me," said Susan. "Let go."

Susie closed her eyes, shaking becoming a full-body shudder that ended when her hands dropped, and she collapsed backward into Susan's arms. Susan was able to catch her niece before she hit the floor, pulling her away from the barrier.

The colors in the barrier stopped swirling, freezing in place for an eye-searing moment before they disappeared and the barrier was nothing but blackness, infinite, deep, and somehow harder to look away from than the colors had been. Susan blinked before she squeezed her eyes shut, snapping, "Harris! Don't look!"

Children could look for longer at a rift without permanent psychological consequences, but that was outside the barrier. There had been no physical effects to rift exposure there, only on this side of the barrier. The rules she'd been studying and trying to define for her entire adult life were different here, on the inside.

There was a popping sound, followed by a rush of air. The crackle of broken wires and flickering lights invaded her ears, along with the distant wail of sirens. Susan opened her eyes.

The barrier was gone.

So was most of the room on the other side. Something had smashed through the ceiling and most of the wall; there was at least one body trapped under the wreckage, leaking blood and viscera onto the floor. Susan stared. There was a rustle as Harris stepped up next to her, and they stared together.

The night sky was on fire, alit with searchlights blazing up from ground level and down from circling helicopters, and more literally, with flames licking up from blazing buildings. Harris swore under his breath. Susan turned to look at him, and kept turning, finally looking behind her.

There was no black haze in the air as Kitty had described; as far as she could tell, they could leave whenever they wanted to. But the room behind them was twisted and blasted, metal bent into terrible new shapes, lines deformed until they formed new angles that defied mathematics, logic, and the eye, refusing to settle into easily visibly lines. The desolation continued as far as she could see. Susan blinked slowly.

"Holy shit," she said.

Susie was a limp weight against her, unmoving. She flinched.

"Angie? Is Susie all right?" It seemed odd to ask one child to tell her the condition of another, but maybe...

"She's not hurt," said Angie, slowly. "Are we home? I didn't think Susie could move people, but I've never seen her make a wall before. Maybe she took us home."

"No, sweetie, we're not at your home. Susie just brought some of what made your home the way it is here."

"She used up all her special and now she's too tired to move," said the boy who wasn't Vincent. Susan looked at him. He frowned and stood, moving toward them. "Do you know what a special is?"

"I don't," said Susan.

His frown deepened. "That's because you're grown. Grown people don't have as much. I don't know why. But there's some. There's another kind of special that only us kids have, and we have it all over us. Angie sees it. She can call more special from where it comes from. I see it too."

"Can you call more?"

He shook his head. "No. But I can move it."

Susan took a sharp breath. She was starting to have a suspicion about what he meant when he said "special." It couldn't be the muons that led them here; the children had a stratospheric level, absolutely, but muons collected on adults at too high a rate. The other particle she'd proposed existing, the one that gave some people abilities they shouldn't have, that had to be what he was seeing. He could see the source of the superpowers.

"Do we have any on us?" she asked.

He cocked his head. "Some," he said, after a long pause. "More than you did before she opened up the hole. Not enough to do anything with."

Susan looked to Harris. She already knew how this ended for her. He met her eyes and nodded, granting permission, and she turned to the boy.

"My friend doesn't need his just-for-kids special," she said. "Take what's on him and put it on Susie."

The boy brightened. "Really?"

"Really," said Harris. "I need to do things here, in this version of the world, and that means I can't go home with you. I don't need it and I don't want it. But I need to be able to go through the barrier to find my godson, so leave the special that's also for adults."

The boy nodded. "All right. This may tingle." He narrowed his eyes, pupils briefly swirling with the same colors they had seen in Susie's.

Harris shivered. There was no way he could feel individual particles moving through his skin, but the imagination is a powerful beast, and in that moment, it seemed like he *could* feel them, like they were being pulled all the way out of his bones.

There wasn't any visual sign of what the boy was doing, not even a glimmer in the air, but Susie sighed and stirred before opening her eyes and blinking up at Susan.

"Did I do it?" she asked. "Did it close?"

Susan nodded. "It did. You did very well, sweetheart."

"I never made one so big before. Mom says I shouldn't do them, because bad things could happen."

Susan looked at the devastation on the other side of the room, the clear signs that something had come through, and sighed. "I think bad things just did."

CHAPTER 49: AFTERMATH

49.1.

Vincent was still unconscious. Harris was tasked to carry him, while Susan took the muon detector in one hand and her niece's hand in the other, and together, the six of them made their way through the ruined office to the street.

Outside, the passage of whatever had come through the rift was much more obvious. Chunks of masonry were missing from the buildings where they belonged and present in the middle of the street, where they didn't belong. Of the cars they passed, none were completely undamaged, although most simply had smashed windows or windshields; only a few had been completely crushed. Susan still held her breath until they found her car mostly intact, save for a brick through the window.

"Harris, Susie sits in your lap," she said. "I doubt the cops are going to be worrying about moving violations tonight, with everything else that's happened, but I want everyone to have a seatbelt, in case everything is still out there, happening to people."

"Got it," he said. The other three children were shepherded, or, in Vincent's case, placed, into the backseat and buckled in before Harris took the passenger seat with Susie.

Susan slid behind the wheel, resting the muon detector and her gun in her own lap. "Everyone in?"

A murmur of assent rose from the backseat, and Susan started the car. Angie gasped. In the quiet that followed, the little boy who wasn't Vincent whispered, "It's okay, Angie. Susie's aunt knows how to make it go."

It hadn't occurred to Susan that the children would only ever have been in a car when they were kidnapped. She pulled carefully away from the curb and started for the freeway. They needed to get to the exclusion zone before anyone realized what had happened.

It was slow going. The streets were in a state of chaos, alarms going off everywhere, cars clogging the road and bodies clogging the crosswalks. Their route partially corresponded with the trail of devastation the creatures had left behind, and in those places, there were fewer cars and more structural damage. Everything seemed to have been designed to slow them down. Susan gripped the wheel and kept driving.

"I know Angie and I know Vincent," she said, pitching her voice to be heard. "But I still don't know you. What's your name?"

There was a sniffle before the little boy said, voice small, "Marcos."

"Well, Marcos, it's very nice to meet you. Thank you so much for your help back there. I really appreciate it."

Another sniffle. "Welcome."

"How did you learn about your 'special'?"

"Everybody in our class has got one. Little sparkles say how strong it's going to be, or what it's going to be. I can see them. Nobody else can except for me and Susie, and she doesn't tell anyone what she can do, and that makes me pretty important."

"Uh-huh." And Angie was a healer, and Susie could open rifts, even though she wasn't supposed to; Susan suspected she'd been taken as an opportunity, not because she'd been targeted. "What about Vincent?"

"He can't see the specials. But he walks through walls and stuff, and it's pretty impressive."

Vincent and Angie would have been enough for any government retrieval team. Susan nodded, shoulders locked tight, but kept her voice light as she said, "Thank you for telling me. I hope he'll wake up soon. I'm very excited to meet him."

"He's nice," piped Susie. "Not everybody has an older brother as nice as me."

"Well, then, it'll be good to be all together as a family." Susan kept driving.

Traffic thinned as they approached the exclusion zone; most of it was heading in the opposite direction, fleeing from the location like it might suddenly spring back to life and start spitting out monsters. Susan swallowed the urge to laugh. No, the monsters weren't coming from Evanston this time. They were in Chicago, they were in the government, they were in tailored suits and boardrooms, making plans about people and profit.

Harris gave her an anxious look. She waved him off, and left the freeway, approaching the checkpoint that would allow them to approach.

She slowed as they neared the fence, rolling down her window and producing her ID. "Dr. Susan Black, Project Tartarus," she said.

"And your friends?" asked the bored guard who took her ID to scan.

"This is Harris Barrie, my graduate student, and my sister's kids." She kept smiling. Marcos and Angie were obviously not white, and Vincent was still unconscious. "Babysitting isn't always convenient."

The scanner beeped. Susan took the gun from her waistband and held it out of sight, between the seat and the door of the car. The man looked at the readout and frowned. Susan's hand tightened on her weapon, but he only nodded and handed her ID back through the window. "Be careful out there, Dr. Black. There was a new rift sighted tonight, and two incursions."

"I will be," she said, returning the ID to her pocket.

Susan pulled forward. Harris gave her a harried look.

"What the fuck was *that?*" he demanded.

"I gambled that General Anderson didn't call the site and tell them to pull my credentials, but we got even luckier than that.

He didn't flag me in the system. That means we have more of a window than I thought."

"My last name isn't *Barrie!*"

Susan laughed, deep and bright and delighted. "Yes, that's the biggest issue."

She pulled up to the exclusion zone itself, the blasted line on the ground, and handed him the muon detector. "Check me."

"What?"

"*Check* me."

Harris blinked several times before pointing the detector at her and pressing the trigger. Then he blinked at the screen. "Your levels have gone up exponentially."

"It was being behind the rift when Susie opened it. We both got a heavy dose today. I can take them home."

She turned off the car and got out, gun in her hand. "Come on, kids. We're going to see your parents. Harris?"

"On it." He got out, moving to retrieve Vincent from the back.

As a group, they approached the barrier. They were almost there when General Anderson's voice rang out from behind them.

"Stop where you are. This is treason."

"And you're alone." Susan turned slowly to face him, raising the gun she still carried. "Did you even ask your men what these kids could do?"

General Anderson's silence was answer enough.

Susan made a disgusted noise and started to turn away.

"Those children are assets of the United States government," he snapped. Gentling his tone, he continued, "This is an arms race and we can't lose. Surely you understand that? We need those children—it's a matter of national security."

"The fact that you're talking this freely tells me you came alone," said Susan. "My niece opened that rift tonight. Any country that engages in this 'arms race' of yours is going to find themselves with much bigger problems than who managed to kidnap more kids for your super-powered army. And these are children, not jets or tanks. *Children.* Did you even know they could breathe out here?"

"I *will* shoot," he snapped.

"You might hit one of the children," said Susan. She started walking again. The others moved with her.

In a very small voice, Angie whispered, "If he deads somebody, I can't fix it. I can only fix what's still alive."

"Then we'll just have to keep breathing, won't we?" said Susan.

The barrier line was just ahead of them. Susan kept walking.

"You're betraying your country," shouted General Anderson.

"You betrayed your country," Susan shouted back. She finally turned back to him. "If you'd told me we had contact, we could have worked *with* Kitty. We could have gotten the children to work with us voluntarily. Now, as a sister, I'll tell you this: the Evanston exclusion zone is no longer yours to exploit, if it ever was. And as a scientist, I'll tell you something else: we have been looking in the wrong places for our answers. You need to stop kidnapping children. Nothing good has come from slavery in all of human history. We're supposed to be better than this."

She looked back to the barrier, and started walking again.

The first bullet hit her just below the ribcage. She shouted and fell, only for Harris to catch her with one arm, almost dropping Vincent in the process. The children moved to shield them with their bodies, and Susan looked up at Harris, face scrunched with agony.

"You have to…go back…" she said.

"I'll sneak out the back," he replied, as lightly as he could. "Come on. We're almost there."

With Susie, Angie, and Harris holding her up, Susan was able to stagger to the barrier. The second bullet whizzed past her head right before she stepped through.

It tingled, but didn't tear her apart. The trees didn't even twitch. Susan smiled even as she collapsed.

"Thought so…" she said. "Muons. Masking us. We belong… here now."

Then everything was blackness, and swirling colors, and she went willingly down to meet them.

49.2.

SUSAN WOKE IN a bed, surrounded by the worried faces of children, Harris, and her sister. There was no pain. She sat up with a wordless sound of joy and yanked Katharine into a hard embrace, crushing the other woman against her.

Kitty was ropey with muscle, strong and lean, and she held Susan back just as tightly, the two of them crying against each other for several minutes before Kitty pulled her face away and said, "Thank you. Thank you."

"Did you know Susie could open rifts?" Susan asked.

"Yes," Katharine admitted. "She's not supposed to, because it's dangerous, but…yes."

"It *is* dangerous," agreed Susan, thinking of the monster or monsters she hadn't seen, and the destruction she had. "But it put us inside a new exclusion zone, and that doused us with enough muons to safely cross the barrier."

"And now you're here."

"And now we're here," Susan agreed. She looked to Harris, suddenly alarmed. "You can't be here! The barrier—"

"Doesn't care about me. Marcos moved the superpowers particle, not the muons. I'm as safe as you are." He smiled wryly, spreading his hands. "Guess I'm still with you, professor."

"Harris, no. We can sneak you out, so you can start looking for your godson."

"I'll have to build a new muon detector. The one we made shorted out when I crossed the barrier."

"Oh, Harris, I'm sorry. I didn't—"

"It's all right," he said, and smiled. "Tomorrow."

"Tomorrow," she said, and hugged her sister again, even tighter. "We have tomorrow. As many tomorrows as we want."

She could teach Katharine everything she hadn't had the time to learn, and she could learn everything the children had to teach. They could smuggle Harris out, and he could find his godson. They could change the world.

Tomorrow.

49.3.

TWO YEARS AFTER the Chicago Incident, the nation of Iceland was destroyed by a series of rifts originating from what was later identified as a government research facility. Of the creatures to come through, three made it into the ocean, and two later went on to attack other coastal nations, killing thousands.

A message was received from the Evanston exclusion zone shortly afterward, consisting of four words:

"I told you so."

Globally, research into the children impacted by the first incident was discontinued, either openly or in private, depending on the country. Tomorrows continued to arrive, one after the other, and in the Evanston exclusion zone and elsewhere, life went on.